Georgia
Under
Water

Georgia Under Water

stories
Heather Sellers

Sarabande Books
LOUISVILLE, KENTUCKY

Managing Editor
Sarabande Books, Inc.
2234 Dundee Road, Suite 200
Louisville, KY 40205

LIBRARY OF CONGRESS CATALOGING-IN-PUBLICATION DATA

Sellers, Heather, 1964–
    Georgia under water : stories / by Heather Sellers.
        p. cm.
ISBN 1-889330-56-6 (alk. paper)
1. Teenage girls—Fiction. 2. Florida—Social life and customs—Fiction.
I. Title.
PS3569.E5749 G4 2001
813'.6—dc21   00-058799

Cover photograph by Sally Gall. Provided courtesy of the artist.

Cover and text design by Charles Casey Martin.

Manufactured in the United States of America.
This book is printed on acid-free paper.

Sarabande Books is a nonprofit literary organization.

Funded in part by a grant from the Kentucky Arts Council, a state agency of the Education, Arts, and Humanities Cabinet.

To Jerome Stern—in memory

Work on this book has been supported by a fellowship from the National Endowment for the Arts. Thanks to Kirby Gann, who read and edited these stories carefully and sensitively. Jane Bach, Jackie Bartley, Sarah Gorham, Jill Heydt, Kate ten Haken, Jesse Lee Kercheval, and Myra Kohsel offer constant support—thank you. For the amazing pre-dawn writing group, I'm indebted to Janis Arnold and Ann Turkle. Deepest thanks to my teachers, especially William Kooistra, Shelia Ortiz Taylor, and Janet Burroway.

Acknowl edgments

Stories in this work were originally published, some in different form, in *Five Points, New Stories of the South, 1999: The Year's Best, The New Virginia Review, Writing Fiction, Alaska Quarterly Review, Chelsea, Arts and Letters,* and *Sonora Review*.

Table of Contents

It's Water, It's Not Going to Kill You   11

Spurt   27

In the Drink   51

Sinking   73

Gulf of Mexico   95

Florida Law   119

Myself as a Delicious Peach   135

Sleep Creep Leap   169

Fla. Boys   193

About the Author   *219*

It's Water,
It's Not Going to Kill You

In the good days, my family lived in a condo, on the twenty-third floor of Pleasure Towers in Ormond Beach, overlooking the Atlantic Ocean.

One afternoon, when we got home from school, my mother was up against the stove, her hands behind her, fingers laced across the cool burners. My father rifled through my mother's orderly Tupperwared leftovers in the fridge, yelling at her, "Why can't you have fun? Why?"

Since I had turned twelve, they'd been fighting. And actually, I noticed, they'd always been fighting. Whenever one walked in the room, the other one was already mad. "I think our parents might be mental cases," I confided to Sid. "I hope no one ever finds out."

Sid thought no one would find out. "They never go anywhere," he reminded me.

"Well, I wish they would," I'd said. "We'd be better off on our own." I had in mind Austrian get-ups, Sid sporting a green pointed felt hat, a cute little house in the woods, lots of pets, newspaper articles on Sid and Georgia Jackson, the amazing fairy tale of two children making it on their own! Here in the heart of Daytona Beach in the middle of 1976!

I stood in the doorway to our galley kitchen, leaning in. But my body was out. I was in. I swung my hips to the side to keep Sid from entering the kitchen, and bent myself into a C in the doorway. They did not see me, their flexible daughter, their daughter in the shape of a good letter.

Sid scooted between my legs and went to the fridge. " 'Scuse," he said.

I could see the ocean between my mother and my father.

I thought he was about to wheel around and hit her.

Get out, I wanted to say.

I realized I was talking to myself.

My brother—Sid—and I were wet in those days, always something of us was wet. Well, me anyway. Sid was dark; he dried faster. My long planks of yellow hair held water like seaweed does—and it was nearly down to the small of my back, where I wanted it—my palms sweated, balls of juice came out of my armpits, and the soles of my feet felt sweet and squishy. Welp, I thought, I'm a girl. Such is my lot.

At night, in the room we shared, Sid would feel the back of my neck, and the wet mats of hair under my topcoat of hair.

"You'll mildew before you're forty," he said. "Your hair is going to rot, you know. You're going to get that crud on your neck, like old people."

"Well, at least I have a brain."

"We should be nice to each other," he said.

"You start first," I said.

Every day, we went from the condo to the pool to the ocean to school, and back, through the pool, up to the condo for cheese and water, and to the ocean, and back for dinner, and then back to the sea until dark.

To Sid, my dark bristly brother, I said, "People will think you're a vermin, and shoot you."

We'd tussle, embarrassed, rolling around on the long white shag carpet; we were too old to be sharing a room, too old to be fighting like dogs, like that.

In my family, the father wasn't supposed to get out of bed before the kids were off to school.

"But don't dads go to work in the morning?" I asked, eating my favorite breakfast, shrimp on toast.

"I get him off after you two are processed," my mother said. She woke us up at six in the morning; we had time to race the elevators (Pleasure Towers had two) down to the Pool Level, dive in, then run down to the beach, and throw ourselves into the cold green sea. Then, we ran across the hard sand, always on the eye-out for shark teeth, raced the waiting elevators, back upstairs, and put our school clothes on.

Our skin could rot off, I thought. But that's the only really bad thing I thought could happen. Or, sometimes, because we never showered, rarely bathed, I thought we might—me and Sid—dissolve. Like maybe it was too much swimming, too much salt drying to powder on our skin, too much lying on the bottom of the pool and watching the sun become a free kaleidoscope, a little too much pulsing with the waves. As though we might stop being children at all.

On Friday at 11:00 A.M. there was another space launch down the road at Canaveral. School was canceled so we could go with our families to see the launch.

"Why not us?" Sid said. We were sitting in the condo. It was late morning, and odd to be on the sofa with my mother. My father's snoring came from their bedroom. My mother's nest of blue blankets was still on the white circular sofa, where she'd slept, curled in the curve of the rented sofa.

"We aren't the kind of family all that interested in *space*," my mother said.

I said, "I'm very interested in space. I am studying the galaxy."

"You aren't," Sid said.

"I want to someday. I want to be a deep-sea diver."

"Then study the ocean, which you don't know anything about."

"It's all related, Sid. Mom, tell him, it's all related."

"Georgia, honey."

"It's all related." I flung myself to the floor and executed a perfect backbend. My shorts pulled up, and I let them, I let the seam tighten between my legs, like I was inside a rubber band. "Tell him!" I felt good and strange, too.

Sid was playing the spoons at the table. My mother drifted to the floor, slunk down. She sprawled out on her side, like a nursery schooler at nap. She put her head down. I sprang onto her.

"Honey," she said softly, not kindly. "I am utterly exhausted. Play with Sid?"

I could see she was exhausted. I could taste her exhaustion. She put her hands over her ears, like I was a shout, just being on her. "I'm too old to play with him," I said.

We'd already been swimming. My braid lay on my back like a wet horse tail. I looked out the sliding glass doors: these were our walls, all along the front and side of the condo—glass walls! I didn't belong here at all. I belonged at the space launch, and not with the kids. I belonged in the rocket. I vowed to start studying the sky. Forget jockeying for the position of keeper of the homonym bulletin board—why was I wasting my time on fifth grade?

"I think we'll go back to Orlando today, use the day to look for housing." My mother was sorting through dozens of paper slips stuffed in her awkward white purse. Her lists.

"No," I said. "Terrible."

"We don't want to move," Sid said. He rubbed her arm. He was nice, like a butler. Like something from *Wind in the Willows*, a beaver or wee weasel of a butler.

"Children," she said. "Please. I need your support."

"Well, what's happening?" I said. I was back on the floor, trying a headstand. "Does he have a new job? Did he get fired, Mom?"

We heard my father clear his throat, or his nostrils, his entire being. Then he launched into a fit of coughing.

My father was between jobs. My mother said we were moving back to Orlando; foreclosure, equity, top-heavy, overdrawn.

"I thought Bethune Cookman was paying for the condo, and he was a teacher now?"

"Ask him, kids. Explain it to your children, Buck."

My dad held his drink in front of her face like a citation.

"Explain it again, please," I said. "You have this money, but you don't?" I didn't feel they were great explainers, even though my mother had been a teacher and my father had been many things.

"Haven't you had this in school? Don't they teach you anything at that goddamn school?"

"Ah," I said, "Yes. Yes. We learn a lot. But you know, it's fifth grade. What can I say?"

"We don't really learn," Sid said. He got a slap on the cheek from my dad. I started sweating between my legs and behind my knees; these were new zones of productivity for me. "Fourth grade isn't really learning." Sid ducked my father's arm this time, and went and sat at the piano, and he pretended to play, dramatically wheeling his hands up and down the keys like a tiny weasel genius.

Mother marched into the dining room and braced herself on the glass table with her arms, as if she were holding that plate of glass down, keeping it from slipping off.

"Yikes," I said.

"You still won't listen," my father said. He kept coming toward her, right up to her face.

"I don't want to listen," my mother said. She pushed her hair back and quickly circled behind the table.

I fell out of my chair. Something I had practiced, fun, like magic tricks or pretending to be drowning, my two other passions in life.

"Georgia," Sid said. He was chewing his hand.

I crawled past them, across the white shag, and folded myself in the credenza.

Sid knocked on the door. Then he stood up and turned his back on the credenza. I felt like I was sailing off.

I sat there crunched up among the tablecloths, the board games, Battleship, Scrabble, Trouble. Usually I felt extremely slender, smart, and small for a twelve-year-old. Sid was eleven, and exponentially smaller. Now I felt huge, an explosion of person.

Hot and huge.

I opened the door to the exact right place. From this vantage point, I had a new view of my family's legs. My father's, bare, because he was in his usual outfit, black dress shoes, thin white socks, and green golfer shorts. It seemed to me his legs were missing a lot of their hair. They were bare, skinny, and shiny, as if he were a woman, or diseased. The skin was pink and spotty, like a leopard shell.

My mother's legs were cricked up under her on the dining room chair. She had her head on the glass; I could see the face of my mother through the glass, crying, squashed, like a sea creature in a too-small tank at the aquarium. My poor mom.

She wore support hose because carrying us two kids inside her body for a total of eighteen months (that's almost two years) caused a serious problem with varicose veins, and she could never again stand for long periods of time. Her legs were hidden in khakis, wrinkled and thick.

Kelly the bird was on top of me, on the credenza. I could hear her eating. I could imagine her tiny legs, those green scales, her knees bending backward as she scratched her back.

"I'm leaving," my father said. In his fed up voice. I heard him pouring a drink.

"Threaten away," my mother said. "You don't scare me. You simply don't." She was up now, looking right at the credenza, not seeing me.

I scratched the inside of the wood. *Grand Rapids, Mich.*, the sticker said. I peeled it off. It was hard to breathe. I ate the sticker.

Sid was on the floor, picking the scab on his knee, making it bleed. He had the pale yellow legs of a blue-eyed person, the skin translucent, and to me—a blonde person with green-brown tan skin—Sid, all pale with dark hair and watery eyes, was creepy. Like a pond at night.

Sid also had white hairs sticking out of his legs. Some like baby hairs and more and more like goat hairs—thick, coarse wires. His legs were noodlelike and difficult to look at for a length of time. He had the scab off in a perfect sheet—I could just feel it between my own fingers like a mat from Mars, a wonderful strange alive/dead thing to pick apart, taste, multiply, save, bury, plant, drop over the edge of the balcony. He had the scab off completely, and he was going around the edge with his mouth, that hard edge. And then the soft middle part would be free. We liked them, scabs.

My father left the room.

"What was that woman doing here?" my mother said through her teeth. Her feet were planted hard in the white carpeting under the inch-thick dining room glass table. "What was she doing here? What was she doing in my house? My house," my mother said.

"Condo," Sid said.

I saw my father's legs reappear.

"MC, you know damn well. You insist on making misery. You fucking insist!" He swatted the chandelier, and one of the teardrop crystals flew into the sliding glass doors. Kelly Green went nuts. I slammed my cupboard door shut and wished I had a pillow in with me, a bolster cushion from the sectional. Then the front door to our condo slammed behind my dad.

I crawled out and had a fit.

I knew I was way too old. I didn't know—something was wrong with me.

Sid brought me a cold washcloth and said he was going down to find shark teeth.

"Wait up," I said. I was trying to breathe again. I had the cold washcloth on my face. I was curled up in a sweaty mess, looking up at the bottom of the dining room table, the smudge mark, where my mother's face had been.

The next night, when my dad told us he was leaving, he put it like he'd been month-to-month the whole time. Like we were leased, and he was moving on.

"I'm giving you my notice," he said. I looked at his watch. It was only 5:00 P.M. My mom and Sid and I were sitting at the table picking the skins of shrimp and drenching them in ketchup. Even my mom liked her shrimp that way, the pink completely dunked in ketchup before she put it in her mouth.

Suddenly there he was, standing behind me, with a lit cigarette, and the dining room—*poof*—silvery with smoke.

I sat at the head of the table, in his seat, by the bowl of shrimp on their big bed of ice cubes in my mom's mixing bowl. Now that we lived at the beach, shrimp was a regular dinner, not such a dressy dinner.

"What about the children, Buck. What about them? I can see why you hate me, and that's fine, that's fine, of course you hate me, but what about them?" My mother kept peeling her shrimp. Now she had a village of them, naked, stranded, small pink hooks all along the edge of her plate.

She wasn't eating. She wasn't moving her lips. Those words—*the children, the children*—came out and hovered with the white and pink shrimpers and the pyramids of translucent shells. And then she toweled her hands, squirted the lemon on them, folded her hands, and seemed to simply put herself away.

I started screaming.

My mother was turning to wax.

Sid said, "We don't need him anyway. He's never here." Sid had popped a shrimp with its shell and tail on in his maw. He was crunching away, and I was so afraid. I was afraid the shrimp would come back to life and swim inside of him. I was afraid my dad was going to wallop him, I was afraid my father would want to marry me and take me with him because my housekeeping skills were so useful and polished, I was afraid I was going to throw up and never like shrimp again.

"Everyone hates you," Sid said.

My dad started to go after Sid with his fist, but Sid was out on the balcony, through the open sliding glass doors, and in about a half a second he was crawling over the railing, hanging there like a monkey on the outside of the railing—I am not kidding. Twenty-three floors up. It wasn't the first time he'd done it, but it was the first time he'd done it real showy like this.

And my mother started screaming, and I thought this was pretty scary, because it was Safety Week and we had learned so much.

If you are on fire, drop and roll. If someone is drowning, don't save them; call someone. One drowning is better than two.

"You all hate me, you hate me," she kept saying without moving a single facial muscle. Then, she did move—she dug at her hair with her hands, pushed her poor hair into one big tall gray fan around her face. I was thinking Madame Tussaud's.

"Honey, come in, come in," she said to Sid. "Get some candy, Georgia," she said. She wouldn't step out there onto the balcony, into the wind. She had never set foot on the balcony.

My dad stood there, his hand in the bowl of shrimp, sloshing them around, sort of stirring the shrimp, the ice.

Sid did banshee screaming. He dropped himself from the balcony, over the other side, and hung on with just his hands. I tried to see if his knuckles were white. Behind him, the Camelot sign was flashing way up the beach, the hotels looked fake like in *Godzilla*, and the sky was wrecked with clouds.

I couldn't believe it. "Sid, come in! Don't mess around!" I yelled.

"*Sh,* you will scare him to his death!" my mother screamed.

"You are the ones making him do this," I yelled right back at her. I wanted to push her. I had to grab my own hands; I had to bite them.

"Shut up!" Sid yelled, and he scooted along the edge, hand over hand, his body hanging over the balcony.

"Fool kid," my father said quietly.

"We should call the fire department," I said. I was frozen, though, to my spot. I looked at the bird. She had her eyes closed. I was envisioning a net, ten men, a bull's-eye, Sid floating, Sid doing somersaults, me on the six-o'clock news. "The pressure cooker that is our family home life got to be too much for him," I could say to the anchorman. People could call and adopt us. We could sleep at the television station and talk to the childless couples who wanted to rescue adorable Georgia and tormented-but-promisingly-sweet Sidley.

My dad made himself another drink in the kitchen, while Mother stood by the sliding glass doors, not going too close to Sid, who still hung. He had his head back, looking up into the dark crazy blue-black sky.

"Mom, don't *push* him. Don't go out there," I said. "That's just what he wants you to do."

"I'm leaving, MC, and you know it's best. There's nothing you can do." My dad spoke from the kitchen. He jangled the car keys. In his other hand, his glass was full and curled close to his chest.

"You are not leaving me, mister. You are not leaving these children. You are not. I will not let you." She shouted this to the balcony.

"I'll come in, Mom. When he goes." Sid faked like he was crawling back over the balcony, and my mom made the sign of the cross and ran through the kitchen and grabbed the car keys straight out of my dad's hands, and ran to the front door and slammed it shut, with her on the inside. She braced herself against the door, a big X.

Sid didn't come in, but I could tell he wanted to. He peered in at us, over the balcony railing. He still dangled, twenty-three floors up. He wanted to see our parents, and he couldn't.

I ran up to my mom, who was gripping her purse and keys in an unnatural way, and the whole time I was hoping my own brother would fall, so at least my parents would have to stay together for my sake, for the sake of the memory of the smushed Sid-man.

I reached for her hand, for the car keys—it seemed to me no one should have them right now. My dad threw his drink down on the carpeting and ripped her off the door, grabbing her behind her neck, and prying her head and back right off. It was like she was wrapping paper. He just threw her down. She landed like pick-up sticks, against the hall table, and the mail there fluttered to the floor.

"You are going about this in the wrong way, MC." She still had the keys. I ducked as my dad swung around, sloshing his drink on my leg, my side, the carpeting, and my mother was up. She took a pouncelike stance. Her eyes were blazing violet. I felt blood in my throat.

"I'll wrong way you, mister."

Then she grabbed her purse from behind the silk bougainvillea, where it was lodged, and she ran out the door for real this time. My dad went out into the hall where we were only supposed to use our whisper voices. He bellowed after her, "There's nothing you can do, MC. I am leaving this cracker factory once and for all!"

But she was the one leaving. She was like a football player running down the red-carpet hall, running to the elevator, her purse tucked deep into her gut.

"You haven't seen anything yet, mister. Let me tell you." The elevator came, and she flung herself in. "You don't know who you are dealing with, buster. If anything happens to these children."

My dad and I tentatively walked halfway down the hall. I wondered if Sid had come in yet. The bronze elevator doors closed around her, and you could see my dad and me reflected all the way down that hall in those elevator doors, only we were tall and thin and wavering, not like real people at all.

"For pity's sake," Dad said. "All hell's broken loose and there's no reason for it to be like this."

I grabbed his leg and cried, *Please please please please please.*

He kicked me. He actually kicked me with his shoe and left a black mark on my thigh. I couldn't believe it.

"Daddy," I was crying. I cried and cried and cried. I couldn't believe how our lives were turning out. I couldn't believe this was my family. I felt this enormous crushing sense. It was never going to be any different. It was never going to be any better. It was never going to be a good family. Suddenly we sprawled in all directions, my family, like a man-o'-war after you poured sugar on it in the sea. Tearing itself apart, as its only way to survive.

I hated Pleasure Towers and the beach, and I was the kind of person who loved the beach. In the hall, slumped up against the stucco-sharp wall, I cried and cried and cried. I hadn't ever cried like that before. I could tell my face would be permanently altered after this cry. I wished people would come out of their condos and rescue me, intervene, but no one did.

"You guys, come quick," Sid yelled. We could hear him way out in the hallway, the tomblike hall of the Towers, and we ran back into the condo, over the thrown-down drink in the hallway, and into the dining room. Sid, firmly anchored on the balcony, chowed down on a super-size bag of M&M's that were supposed to be for baking, not eating. He stood there, popping them in, staring down at the beach, like he was at the races.

"Look," he said, and pointed toward the beach.

At the edge of the water, our aqua blue Plymouth was about to be launched.

My mother was driving it into the water. Some flares glowed on the beach behind her; I don't know how they got there.

Our family's car was slowly drifting into the Atlantic Ocean, my favorite body of water.

"Daddy," I whispered. "Oh, no."

Then it stopped in the sand that is soft right before the wave sand. She hopped out. Her ankles were in the breakers, her support hose would be getting wet, carrying that water up her legs—it was too awful to imagine. Beside her, the station wagon bobbled, nosed, settled.

"For God's sake," my dad said. "You don't get an engine wet. Is she out of her mind?" He threw his cigarette over the edge. Sid watched it float down and made bomb noises the whole way.

"*Sh*," I said. I didn't want a lot of freak-out movement up here. I didn't think we should be distracting my mother. Pushing her over the edge. She motioned the people clustering behind her on the beach to get back, get back, her white vinyl purse clutched like the space capsule she was taking to Atlantis, the lost city, and she hopped back in and hit the gas; the Plymouth lurched and launched and went out, farther, into the water.

"Oh, Jesus Christ, she has to do everything the goddamn hard way," my dad said. He wasn't going to be able to leave us, though; you have to give my mom credit for that. What could he do, walk?

"Sid, son, get your ass off the railing, son." He slammed his drink down his throat. Now that Sid stood with us, inside the balcony, his upper body flopped over it, my dad suddenly got parental. I wanted to say that, but I knew I'd get hit. Plus, I had the altered face from my big cry a few minutes ago, and it hurt to talk. And, my mother had just driven our car into the Atlantic Ocean. I didn't want to get sent to my room at this juncture.

People gathered in greater numbers to watch our ocean-borne Plymouth. Buffy from the twelfth floor of our building, and Angie, the gate man's daughter, were there. A few dog walkers and the usual retired men in sweaters and brown bathing trunks clustered in small groups. The car kept going out. Bobbing like a toy. The ocean, I pretended, was a bulletin board, and my mother, a friendly felt object, and we could pin her anywhere; the ocean was tiny. "Okay," I said, cheerily. "She'll come back now. She'll come back. It's getting dark, almost." Mentally, I pasted her and the wagon onto the sand, like felt pieces on a pale fabric board.

"We should go help her out, man," Sid said. "It's a scene."

A man with white hair, a guy who looked like Santa, waded in after the car and waved his arms in the *rescue me rescue me* SOS signal.

When the breakers hit, the car nosed up, then down. Angling down, it lost ground—that is, from our point of view. It came back toward shore—a good two waves' worth. Everything seemed about to be okay; the car easing back to the beach, the windows rolled down. She could get out. I knew she wouldn't leave her purse.

"She won't leave her purse," said Sid.

Sid peeled fronds off the palm on the balcony, my dad drank deeply, and I just sat there, bars of the railing between my toes. I felt like I was watching television.

"Could I have a sip of that?" Sid asked our dad. Sid stood fully planted inside the balcony now. Not hanging over. Now I had the urge to push him over. My mode made me angry: when Sid got into danger, I wanted to rescue him. I wanted the wind to be perfectly still when he hung over the edge of the balcony, or sat on the rail, barely balancing. I couldn't even breathe. But when he stood all military-proper on the AstroTurf, begging my dad for a sip of his liquor, not even watching Mom in the Plymouth, I wanted to shove him off the twenty-third floor. I wanted Sid to be arrested and for us visit him at Boy's Town. There would be organized activities, and I would visit so often I would become the Dean of Boys when I grew up, and kids everywhere would want to come to this place, to be in my command, to be safe from their parents. I could learn to sew, I thought, and I wanted to jump off the balcony. Why did I have a brain like that? Who wanted to save their family and kill their family at the same time?

But when we were all scattered like this, I wanted us to be back like we were, although I couldn't remember what that would have been.

Some of the men on the beach had waded in, but they stood way off, leeward, out of the way. You couldn't tell if the men were talking or not. You couldn't tell if they had a plan. And she was still in the car; at least I think she was. Had she swum away? Had she somehow slipped into the water and swum to the bottom of the sea? The light was getting shifty and blue-black, most of the peach streaks all gone, and I couldn't see my mother anymore. Was she lying down on the front seat?

Two dogs broke loose and raced each other to the car. But the light looked different, and everything was flat and unreal, like a movie, though I had never actually seen a movie. My mother would not be rescued because this was not an accident. It was on purpose.

Sid was now back to straddling the balcony like it was a horse. My dad pretended to shove him.

"Jesus, Dad, kill me why don't you."

"Are we going down there? What are we going to do, Daddy?" I asked. I tried not to sound whiny. "Shouldn't you—"

"—Fuck her," he said. "We are going to fuck her."

With that the car turned sideways and lunged back toward us, back to the sand, the shore, the tiny miniature onlookers in their dark bathing suits; all catawampus our family car hooked itself back onto the beach and rested on the sand sideways, listing.

The three of us stood on the balcony like the Swiss Family Robinson without the Swiss part, without the Robinson part. We were just up high. And we huddled by Sid, my dad's glass of vodka gleaming like a steady light, my hands around his waist. I pressed my stomach into his back so my guts wouldn't launch. Slowly, as the seawater turned pink all around the aqua blue Plymouth in the last streaks of sunset, she climbed out of the window on the driver's side and came back at us.

Spurt

One day in the middle of being thirteen years old, living the high life in our condo, complete with a heat lamp, cigarettes, and a wraparound balcony, overlooking the lovely Greater Daytona Beach area and a slice of the ocean—I had it.

My growth spurt. Between Saturday and Tuesday, the first of July, my legs dropped out of my body and became long sleek noodles. My legs were so lovely, I couldn't keep my hands off them. I shaved them; it took an hour. I knicked myself, toilet-papered the cuts, and then rubbed the long legs with cocoa butter from my father's medicine cabinet. He had strange oils, Old Spice, and enemas. Fleet, "Number one in nursing homes," it said. I read the directions to everything.

I felt guilty using his Sensual Tan Hawaiian Cocoa Butter Plus

Aloe Vera, but it smelled so good, it was so thick and white, I couldn't stop pasting it all over my glorious extended legs and rubbing, rubbing it in.

I shaved before school, after school; when I swam in the ocean, my legs burned like I wore chaps of thorns. At night, in my bed, Sid yakking that the lotion stank and made him puke, I rubbed lotion on my thighs, under the covers. I pretended various boys from school were the rubbers. Once I pretended the doorman did it. I could hardly sleep, I swear to God, with the new legs. They were simply too beautiful, too much perfection.

During this phase, I pretended I was a religious figure. I practiced, diving into the breakers, screaming silently. My freshly shaved legs burst into swaths of red dots. I baked in the sun, with Sid throwing sandballs and shells at me, until the inflammation subsided. I tried not to lie on my breasts; I kept myself propped up when I was back-tanning. I wanted the breasts to be so much bigger. They were already bigger than my mother's. I wanted them to be like my father's lady friend's. I wanted them to be moving in the direction of the Dolly Parton ideal—the boys at school couldn't stop talking about her: bras, nipples, size.

One day Mike Partain said to me, "Hey, thunder-thighs." It was confusing because I liked him saying that, and I also wanted to hide under the bottlebrush tree and not come out until I was adult.

But for now, I had legs, and I was five foot eight inches tall, the second tallest girl in my class. The tallest girl, Cindy Sides, had acne villages on her face and arms and chest. She gave tall its reputation for *freakish*. The smallest girls were most popular—tight, proportioned, fit, little fiddlelike girls—Nancy Nation, Julie Harrington, and Carrie Cicone to be specific. They were what my mother, who was petite herself, called petite. Yuck. I was tall in the friendly tree way, and I could tell my legs were going to turn out to be my best feature. They already were. I was a blonde leggy babe.

I spent those days watching myself in every reflective surface known to Daytona Beach.

My knees weren't knobs anymore. My knees were lush transitions. My thighs shone golden-brown; my shins, paler, but long and strong. My ankles were slim, bony in a fetching way, my feet suddenly inches too long for my slaps and sandals. My hair swung in a shiny curtain behind me; my legs were in constant motion, counterpoint.

"You've had a growth spurt," my mother said. "Your shorts are way too short. When did this happen?"

"I think yesterday and/or the day before," I said. We were in the parking lot of our condo, waiting for my father to return with the wagon. It was windy, and the world smelled like fish, strong muscular fish.

"This wind!" she said. She clamped her hands on her head. I stood behind her, to protect her from blowing down to Ft. Lauderdale.

I was so much taller than she was. "Mom," I said. I looked at her dirty white sneakers, her khaki jumpsuit, her aqua kerchief, her watery fading eyes. She had stray bobby pins hanging off to the side of her forehead. Her lips were thin and pale. She was missing a snap at her throat. The fabric was torn and white there, like you could see the cells of the khaki work suit. "I'm way too tall for you." I made her stand up against me, so she could feel where her head hit mine. I did cheat, but I didn't need to—I was much taller. "I can't wear your clothes, Mom. That would feel weird."

"Well, you've had your growth spurt. I'm telling you." She moved away, looked around the corner of the stucco building—a red race car zoomed through our lot—not my pop. "The day is wasting," she said. She leaned into the wind.

We walked to the 7-Eleven and got the Yellow bus to the grocery store for our weekly pick-up. I sat in the second to last seat, next to a man with a pile of newspapers and a huge plastic garbage bag all poked out with stuff. "How do you know?" he said to me.

"I don't," I said. I could see the back of my mother's head. She was communicating to the driver. We lurched along, and I stared out the window, letting it vibrate my cheek, like a dentist or lover.

School was out for the summer, the summer of 1977. Already I was sick of reading biographies, novels, and *House Beautiful*. I was between selves—not a clue what might interest me next; my mind felt vacant as the beach. I did have a hankering for a pair of flag short-shorts. A white string bikini. Some barefoot sandals. My own apartment.

I trotted after her, looking at my new legs, their sunny length, their smooth curves, the place where the thigh went inside the shorts. I stared at them everywhere: the fronts of the refrigerator units, the mirrored strip along the meat counter, the shiny fronts of the deli cases. She handed me packages of meat, and I watched myself putting them into the cart.

Oh, my legs. My luscious legs. When I thought no one was looking, I leaned over the cart, rearranged the milk, the juice, the bread with one hand, and gave each of my nipples a hard pull. One of my more daring moves. Sid had told me that the Pereddie boys had told him they had a code for braless T-shirted women, women in bathing suits, and particularly hideous women. I could imagine the intercom: Joe, there's a 6-52 in Aisle 11. Joe, 6-52, Aisle 11, and then a stampede of bag boys to Aisle 11.

"Honey!" My mother shouted at me in frozens. "The cart! My purse!" I'd been staring at myself in the shiny vinyl doors to the refrigerators, the employee part, and completely spaced out. Our cart had been temporarily adopted by a man with a walker, Now it sat parked at a precarious tower of baby food.

"Does your brother still want frozen pizza, or is he not eating those anymore?" She stood close to the freezers, rubbing her shoulders and tapping her foot. Her face was crinkled up, and she stared hard at me, like I was keeping information from her on purpose.

"How should I know?" I shrugged, and slid down the aisle, where I noticed the Coke machine's shiny Plexiglas front panel would reflect my legs. I loved them. I wanted to continue to have this growth.

"Does he eat Slim Jims? Georgia?"

I pretended not to hear this person, the walking nervous breakdown. I pretended to consider a Coke purchase.

As we finally got into a lane she liked she said, "I don't like this new way you are walking. You look like you are trying to push your bottom out, Georgia. As though you are trying to draw attention to yourself." She talked loud, as though there weren't *other people* in the aisle at all. I picked up an Archie comic and smiled shyly, up and over, at a blond surfer guy, his arms piled high with bananas. He was cutting through the closed lane next to us—seemingly just walking out of the store with all those bananas. It made me laugh. That was someone I could marry, I thought. As he passed, I could smell the sweet salt on his skin.

"Hey," he said, and he hiked himself over the guard rope, and the bananas didn't even move.

"Wow," I said.

"Georgia," my mother said. "Unloading." She banged the cart back at me, nudged me. "Please? Honey? Dear?"

"Yeah, yeah."

My mother was just a quiet skinny shy person, and I was going to be very different; I was more ruler material. A queen's future I saw for myself. A presidential invitation. Photos, dresses, and people—everyone staring at me, stranger and family member alike.

The bag boy, Joe Pereddie, a pointy-elbows and greasy-dark-hair kid, was not the sharpest pencil in the drawer. I'd heard a teacher say that about him. I wanted to say it about someone.

I squeezed past my mother while she went through the coupons with Marge the cashier. I stood by Joe, just because that's where you stood. His stubbly face reddened brusquely while I waited by him.

My mother wrote out a check for the groceries. I didn't want the glorious beach boy to see me, with my legs, standing next to Joe Pereddie.

"Ma," I said. I made a rolling hands, *let's go*, motion. "This lifetime?"

"Eh, hey, how's it goin', man," Joe said to me.

I pretended, for a long moment, that I didn't hear. I looked all around, 360 degrees, for a reflective surface. I needed to see what this looked like, Georgia Jackson, long blonde thick wild unbrushed hair, long tan legs, like highways, cute shorts, nice butt. I needed to see her, talking to Joe Pereddie, I needed to see what it looked like. "Oh," I said. "It's going, you know. Summer. Boring?"

I looked pointedly into our grocery bags and could feel him reddening all over again. "So," I said. "Yeah." I hiked myself up on the metal railing and slung my legs back and forth. "Ma," I said.

I felt like Marilyn Monroe or a French woman of some kind. I piked my left leg, and then extended and flexed my right.

Mom chastised me all the way back to the apartment, but I didn't care. I had liked talking to three actual males—it was an important day for me; the first time I had ever remotely enjoyed Publix with my mother. She'd never understand. I sat slumped in the front seat of the bus with her, our groceries heavy in our laps.

"You've become very vain. You are show-offy, and proud. You don't understand, people don't like girls to be overly—"

"Hey yourself," I'd say next time. That was so cool. "Hey yourself," I whispered as we got off at our stop. "Hey to you too."

"Where have you been?" she said when my father came home that evening.

"Can we still go to the fireworks?" Sid asked.

"I can't take it anymore." My mother slumped against the wall of the dining room. "I just can't. The worry—it's too much. I'm losing my health."

I sat by her, but she pulled away.

"Mom," I said. "I'm good."

"You think—" she said, and glared as though I wasn't even me. I looked at myself in the chrome of the dining room table's base. I was elongated and wiggly, peculiar in the chrome legs, a funhouse effect. I wanted to cry, and I wanted to pull her hair and hug her. "You think everything is about you and your—"

"Mom!" I said. I jumped up.

"Let's go, kids. We can still have fun." My father was loading the little red cooler with a six-pack of Old Milwaukee. Sid carried the cooler for us, and the three of us went down to the beach. My dad was wearing his too-small green bathing suit, black dress shoes, and a large floppy white hat of my mother's.

My father sat ensconced with his beer, down on the beach by Sid's hut. I wrestled Sid under the waves and pretended to drown him. "He's in Davey Jones's locker," I yelled up to my dad in the sand. I waved my father to come join us in the ocean. My dad had two beers lined up in pits by his towel on the beach. It was chilly; my arms and ears were cold.

"Great, Georgia," he yelled back, his words lost in the wind. "Go for it." I could read his lips. They were shiny, thick, like a camel's. I held slippery Sid under my feet, under the waves.

I didn't want him to die. But I couldn't let him up until he was mad enough to attack me. It's so strange, being in a family. We're nice to anyone, as long as we don't know them.

My dad stared off at the plane dragging past the beach, low in the sky, with its ad for a tourist bar: EAT SHUCKERS RAW. I towered over Sid in the surf and looked away from my dad and his beer friends. *Great, Georgia?* I thought. *I'm killing your son.* I finally let Sid up. Sid dug his fingernails deep into my new silky taut skin, my gorgeous thighs, drawing blood, but he couldn't push me down. I was too tall. I jumped Sid again, my bathing suit sliding around like little flags in the wind.

Around us there were cars with boys on the hoods, and the music of Bruce Springsteen and Cat Stevens and Aerosmith braced the black-pink air. I took a walk. I walked down to the pier, where they were loading the fireworks onto a black barge. I was barefoot and tiptoed past hooks and lines and dead fish and pop-tops. I walked about halfway to the gate, at which point you had to pay. I watched the surfers. There was one girl on a slender green board. I walked down to the Holiday Inn. Rich girls sat in striped canvas cabanas. I wished to be invited to join their parties, but I wouldn't have, even if they'd said, *Hey, come on in! Have a daiquiri and sit by me!*

My legs were streaked with aches—I'd walked maybe longer than I had ever walked in my life. I'd been gone a long time.

People don't know this, but you can get sunburned in the rain, in the evening, underwater, even fully dressed. So when I got back to my dad, I woke him up. His skin had that look—taut and white—that tells you the burning will begin tomorrow.

I slouched between his legs, leaning back on his sandy scratchy chest, enjoying the fireworks over the ocean. Lights of boats stranded the water like jewelry.

"Oh," I said, "I'm in heaven." I folded myself into him more, and wondered if our mother was watching. "Sid," I said. "Get over here!"

Someone nearby yelled, "Dude!"

The fireworks, pink chrysanthemums, sprinkled down into the ocean, seeming to kiss and dust the boats. My father said, "If only the rest of the family was here. I wish they could have a good time. They could enjoy the spectacle of it all."

I scooched down deeper into the cool sand. I partly wished I was buried in it.

His breath was sour, but I let it itch away at my neck. He was my dad. I knew he was odd and fine, brilliant, crushed. He was my father, Buck Jackson, a man without a plan. I loved him with my entire being and my entire heart—when I thought of my father, when I lay back on him, in the warm sticky nest of him, the two of us an island on the beach, my hair slapping his arms and face, the night around us like a big scary blanket, I could feel every single cell in my aorta, and it hurt. That's how much I loved him.

"I said where is everybody?"

A pink pelican showered from the sky down into the crisp ocean. It was cold now, and my father's skin was that hot-freezing of burned skin. I pretended I couldn't hear him. I pretended I was a tiny baby, just getting my first start in life. A sprout, the cutest thing.

"They'll be down. I think Sid's right over there in the stink hut. They're seeing it, Daddy," I said quietly. "They're seeing it from where they want to be, is all."

The next day, I went back to the grocery store, by myself. I rode Sid's bike and left it, unlocked, at the curb. I got a cart.

I hiked myself up on the rail and kick-pushed along, down the aisles. I watched my legs, reflected in the strips along the bottom of the shelves. I watched my bottom, cute in bee-print shorts, shapely in the mirrors behind the meat department. I hung out in fruits for a while.

"Hey," the blond kid said.

I felt sick. Like I had stolen food. I had only been looking. I wasn't even close to hungry. I was just following my cart. I looked down; it was empty. I felt so dumb and also very brave.

"Want to go out back?" he said. I looked at his eyes for just a sec. It was the banana-carrying boy from yesterday. He was in a green apron; he worked at Publix after all.

"Pardon?" I said. I let the cart slide away from me. It had become a crutch. It bumped into the melons display, squeaking. "You said?"

"I have a break. You wanna—"

I didn't want to. "Yeah," I said. I looked at how my feet and his feet were all in green tiles, not in white tiles. "Sure, yeah."

He jerked his head, so I knew to follow him. Under his apron, he was wearing a thin tank top, the kind we weren't allowed to wear to school. He was so tan, his skin looked like carpeting, deep brown carpeting. His blond hair was frosty from the sun, white streaks in the shiny gold. He had a big head, broad shoulders, and a slow easy walk. He smelled so good—like bananas and salt and wood.

The black plastic flap doors to the produce inner sanctum closed behind me with a *thwack*.

He didn't hear me. A couple of older men in white aprons were sweeping; one was on a ladder. "What's up, Kyle," one said.

"Dude," Kyle said.

"What's this?" one of the men said. Kyle flashed him a peace sign. We jumped out of the back of the store, off the loading dock, and then I followed him to the edge of the dirt-sand driveway, to where the orange grove started and Publix stopped.

He told me to sit on an orange crate. "Firm enough?" he said. He smiled. His eyes—I just wanted to look at them, hold them in my palms and really take them in. He smiled even more, and scooted his crate close to mine, and lit a cigarette. "Smoke?" he said.

"Yeah," I said. "But not right now."

"Relax," he said. His teeth were white and perfect, big. "Everything's cool. So, you go to Ortona High, or what?"

I felt odd without my cart.

"So," I said. I crossed my legs, and that action somehow toppled me over, from my crate, off the back of it. I felt my thigh tear—a nail raked across the top, up by my shorts, and my skin was scratched—the second day in a row of bleeding legs.

"Whoa," he said, after I got up, brushed myself off.

I licked my finger and erased the skid of blood. "Shoot," I said. "I'm such a klutz. Obviously." I laughed, loudly, and felt as though I had not a head on my neck, but a large gaping space, filled with odd gasses. "Oh," I moaned and touched my finger to my nose.

"You're a shy girl," he said. "That's cool. Where do you go to school, I haven't seen you in classes, man." He sucked hard on his cig and flicked it into the orange trees. He stood up. I thought he was going to kiss me. But he was grinning, like a lion, or a baby, some creature of good niceness.

I couldn't answer. I wrapped my legs one around the other and stood on one foot knotted up like that. I couldn't tell him I was in junior high; he thought I was much older. I couldn't get my tongue off the roof of my mouth. I wanted a piece of fruit.

I kicked at the oyster shells and ashes in the center of the loose circle of crates. My head felt like it was pitching forward, like it would take off, taking his head with it. I was so sweaty. I started to cry.

"Oh, hey, man, hey, dude," he said softly, and he reached to put his arm on my shoulder. I felt if he touched me, I would burst into flames.

I ran, not through the store, but around the alley. My flatbacks were tripping me up, and I kicked them off and ran fast across the sand and shells and stickers. Some boys whooped. I don't know if he did.

I rode home barefoot, the metal teeth of the pedals reminding me I couldn't ever ever ever just be a simple person, I was a girl, I was Buck's daughter.

We shared a room, the only drawback of my swanky, seventh-grade growth spurt life. Sid was in this phase where he was always pretending to be a snoring screamer monkey. That particular night I was not going to be able to sleep though the brouhaha. The sky was so bright with all the hotels and searchlights, the constant party of Daytona Beach. Sirens came in through the sliding doors, and the ocean hummed, slapping softly. I didn't want to grow up any other place than Florida. I felt sorry for all other girls. I hooked my toes to the end of the bed and stretched myself taller by hanging onto the wicker headboard with my pinkies. I twisted in my father's T-shirt, the only thing I'd wear to sleep in.

I could hear the television on in my father's bedroom. *Hogan's Heroes.*

"Sid. Sid. I know you're awake. When did they start sleeping not together?" I fanned my sheet over my body, like I was an Arabian mistress.

"Please shut up, George," he said. I could smell his breath, his ten-year-old Tang breath. It was that stuffy in our condo. I grabbed my lotion from the nightstand between our beds and started rubbing my legs down again. I'd already done it once tonight. But the cocoa butter soothed my scars.

"That smell makes me puke. You're kind of sickening me," Sid said. "Why don't you just use slobber?"

"Are they getting a divorce? Have you overheard anything, or seen anything, like legal papers?" Under the sheets, I squirted out more cocoa butter and put on another coat. I thought of my dad's poor burnt husk—someone should be rubbing him.

"Damn," I said. "Crap." I was trying to conjure up a bad mood, a terror. I sat back on my bed, bouncing my hips on it, like I was riding a horse.

"Please, shut up," Sid said in snore language.

I shook my sheet, sending the lotion smells over to him, full blast.

"God, George," Sid said. He got out of his bed. I couldn't bear to look at him in his underwear. The kids of Pleasure Towers knew we shared a room—how did they know that? "Y'all kiss, y'all kiss," they said when we saw them down at the pool. "*Oooh.* Incest is best." They said this whenever they saw us. I turned red and fled to the bottom of the pool, where I'd just hold my breath. They'd get out, and go over to the shuffleboard court, and stand in a huddle like gulls until Sid and I were done in the pool and went our separate ways up and down the beach.

"Wanna go outside? The other day, I walked down to the Holiday Inn. We could sneak in their pool. Remember we were going to do that?"

He didn't answer. Ever since he'd built that hut it was like he was a different person. A hut-dweller. A little darker, and a lot less fun.

Wearing my sheet like an empire princess, wrapped tight around my poor sore breast buds, I flung the sliding glass door open, wide, and all the salty wind came in, and the carnival of noises from Saturday night on the strip, A1A, below.

I went out to the balcony, and sat down on the green AstroTurf.

Sid got cigarettes out from under his pillow. They weren't in a package, just loose, like soldiers, flattened, slightly bent, and silly-looking in his pale palms. He offered me one, but I told him I had been smoking too much lately.

In the next room down, I could hear my father hacking away like he was about to die. His sliding glass doors were open, his aqua drapes closed, and they flapped in the wind. There was always a wind, up this high. A wind with edges on it.

Sid couldn't get anything lit. I tried to block the wind for him with my sheet, without exposing myself.

"I wished I had a really nice brother. Or no brother." I said this softly, to the zigzag part of his black hair.

"Stop," I said. "You are a horrible little person."

"What, don't like the smell of burning flesh?"

"Not really." I wondered if my mother would see the light of his cigarette out here.

"I'm hatching a plan," I said.

"God, George, please please don't talk like that. You sound like a complete idiot. You sound sick. I'm telling you. For your own good. Don't talk like you are in the Hardy Boys. Ever." Sid sat cross-legged on the AstroTurf like a tiny swami. His white underwear like swaddling something or other. He looked about twenty-five years old. "*Eee, vee, eee, ar.*" It completely horrified me to see that underwear, the Y of it, the pocket in the front, the black and mustard stripes of the elastic. It was something I never wanted to get near.

"But do you want to hear it?"

"No, I'm thinking about going on a killing spree personally. Do you like killing sprees?" he said.

I wrapped up into my sheet tighter. I put one length of the selvage edge in my mouth, that long band there like a hard worm between my teeth.

"Why not? A killing spree can be fun for the entire family!"

"We have to go and sleep with them. They'll leave us otherwise. They are getting ready to leave us. Can't you see anything? Did you see Dad on the beach today? He said he was divorcing Mom," I said, trying this out for the sound.

"Fuck no," he said. He threw the cigarette—even though there was plenty of it left—into the wind. It came right back at us, and I ducked and winced. "We're not stopping them. Do you know that that would be...whatever that would be."

"Just please believe me," I said. I knew my father didn't want to stay in this family. I didn't blame him. My mother was not even cooking anymore. She never even left the condo, except for Tuesday at 7:00 A.M. to go to Publix to buy the exact, I mean exact same things again. She was afraid of everything. She just froze him out when he was home, and he almost never was; he was gone for days and days on end. She kept her purse in the oven, and she lay perfectly still and pale and see-through, like a dead ghost crab, on the sofa all day and all night. It was strange. And, when he was home, he lay out on the balcony outside his room, naked, completely, "going for the allover tan."

In the mornings I would get Sid out of bed, and we'd eat cereal just plain on the balcony, and then we'd go to the sea with sandwiches in plastic bags, and I would give us instructions to stay in shallow water, come back for dinner.

Sometimes I would stand by the coffee table and stare down at her forehead, sort of looking inside her.

"Where's your brother going?" she'd say, if she said anything.

"I burned my penis again today," my father would say, if he was there at dinner. Sometimes he boiled shrimp for us.

"We are in the middle of a viscous circle," I said to Sid. "We have to do something. We have to try." I could tell I was sounding like Anne of Green Gables again, and that this would drive Sid over the edge.

Sid was still smoking, on his third of the slender damaged cigs.

"Can I have taste?" I said.

"Like hell you want to," he said. "Georgia. I wasn't going to tell you. But I'm going to, okay? I'm leaving. I'm going to San Antonio. I'm not coming back. Don't expect me." His nose shiny, and his voice all straight lines and even.

"Just go be with her. I'll tuck him in."

"Oh, incest is best," he said. I wasn't even exactly sure what that word meant, but I knew, like you know not to eat certain things you might find in the water or even in your own refrigerator—I knew *enough*.

I said, "You look like an ape."

"Apes kill people," he said. He started lunging on my head, pressing his groin into my face, and pummeling my back as he looped over me. I saw the street below as I tried to crawl away; I looked through the railing and told him I was going to vomit. My legs were long enough to reach the wall, and I tried to grip, hang, press myself away from the edge, to the wall; Sid was so much stronger than I was. I screamed, and I could hear my father roar from his Master Suite. The Johnny Carson show was to the singing part, the music part.

"What's going on?" he said in his late-night slurry voice.

"Okay, okay, okay, get off me—" I bit Sid hard on the ankle. He was horrible and hairy and tasted like dead gum.

"Hey, hey. Let's cut it out, man." He bopped me on the head, then grabbed my shoulders, and I thought *he wants to kiss me*. It was like being in a parking garage. I wanted to slam out of there and go faster than you are allowed to go. Just because it is a parking garage. "I'm really leaving, Georgia. Just so you know."

"Right," I said. "I'll come with you. This place is crazy. They are totally nuts. I just want to get married and get out."

"Don't be stupid, Sis," he said. That was what he said to me.

I stepped aside.

I could hear my mother moan as Sid got out there, probably feet to head on the couch with her. They could talk all night.

After a bit of breathing in the night air and watching men walk up and down the Strip of Daytona, and then disappear down onto the Boardwalk in the hot windy night, I decided it was time for me to do my part to keep this family together. Tiptoeing, I entered the Master Suite from the balcony, beating the drapes with my palms so they scalloped around me like robes, entering part princess, part fish caught in a net, and tripped over my father's dress shoes. He was still there, exactly as he had been, bottle of vodka on the nightstand, his body parked dead center in the mushy king-size bed. He reminded me so much of a *Gulliver's Travels* episode. He had a glass, an amber glass, on his belly, and his hand kept it there, though he was asleep. Just give him an I.V., Sid was always saying.

I swept past him, letting my gown sheets swirl effectively, half nurse, half queen, and I swished into the giant gold tile and black Formica bathroom and turned on the red heat lamp, which I always did when I came back in here. My mother had made the room off-limits. The forbidden room, with the forbidden sleeping man, lurked back here, like a box of Pandoras, a place within our condo where the adult doings of my father, his mysterious comings and goings, late nights, brown grocery bags of bulky what? And alcohol, the television, the radio, the sun lamp—everything forbidden in our lives was in this room.

I thought about laying out, naked, locking myself in the forbidden bathroom, but instead, I gathered my sheets around me, and I went to his side. I pounced on the edge of the bed. I kept my sheets wrapped tightly around me. The entire mass of bed and father shifted my way, and he lifted his hand in the air, pink, pudgy, as if it had been marinating in whatever was back here, whatever potent sticky substance you could smell in the air even now—a smell of man, loneliness, beer, sugar, blue television. He batted at me blindly and snored. Mucus hung in his mustache. As if he were caught in a spider web that emanated from his own body.

I grabbed his pawing hand and put it on his stomach. He looked like a corpse, so I got up on my hands and knees and pushed one arm off his stomach. It landed on the mattress like a dead fish, a big fish. I kneeled over him, letting my sheets show off my terrific new cleavage, and ministered to his other hand, *let me just make you more comfortable.* I licked the inside of his wrist. Stay, I whispered. I was a hypnotist. If he woke up, he would see me as a vision, an angel, a girl-Houdini-type person. I licked his arm again. The taste was metal and salt and bitter and hairy. I held his arm and breathed on it, whispering a fakey incantation.

I made myself ignore what was awful, and I loved him. I didn't think anyone else did. I thought of Kyle, and Marge, and the beach girls, and the fish guys. They'd do the same thing. I wasn't going to turn into the kind of person who let a drowning man go. I pressed up against him and continued with the hypnosis. *Stay stay stay stay stay,* I said, licking his wrist. *Stay.*

He rolled away from me a bit and upset his ashtray, a giant green plastic pontoon in the middle of the ocean of bed. Ashes flurried in the air, settled against his body, perfumed the area with smoky smells of stale man. I leaned over him, letting my body graze his, and pulled the ashtray out from where it was wedged under him.

So I went back into the bathroom to empty and wash that ashtray. It was an inferno in there—I'd left the sun lamp on. It clicked away on its timer, like a bomb, like cookies in the oven. The room glowed red. My skin looked purple. My blonde hair looked black. The mirrors, lining all the walls and the ceiling, too, were marbled, veined with gold, and they reflected the black/red/green light thousands of times over.

The faucet came out only on high blast, and the ashes were everywhere. Like Pompeii, they coated the counter, shuddered on the carpet, stuck to the mirrors, my arms, my gowns. I closed the bathroom door, leaving it for someone else to deal with, and crawled on my hands and knees to the bed. The carpet burned through my gowns, burned my knees. Why this woke him up I do not know.

"What the hell are you doing in here, Georgia?" he sounded furious and violent. He put his hands over his eyes and sat up against the headboard, the whole bed wiggling like jelly. This was not a quality mattress; my mother was right. And I loved it, the marshmallow joy of its hug. I crawled up there with him. And knelt beside him and stuck out my tongue, I do not know why.

"Please let me sleep with you, please hold me," I said.

"Get in your own room," he said. I jumped on top of him and laughed, pretended to ride him like when I was young and we played horse and rider, and he smacked me on the cheek.

"Pops," I said. I didn't get off him. I sat straddling him, feeling very strange worms in my stomach and lower intestines. Like I might throw up or I might be getting really hungry. I could not tell. I pushed up and down again, to get him to talk, to get him to do something else, not the slapping, rewind, do over. "Daddy, guess what." I shook him and bounced. He didn't respond at all. I ran my fingers across his crazed eyebrows, settling some of the wildest wires back into the general region. "Daddy," I hissed. "Guess what. Don't tell Mom. But I have a kind-of boyfriend. I have a boyfriend now." I let my tongue feel the letter K and wondered what his last name was.

"Why I am being disturbed in my rest, I do not know," he said, full volume. "God, what a day, what a day," and he blew his nose right into the sheets—I don't know which one, his or my gowns. His head did not seem centered over his body. He blinked his eyes and focused on me, straddling him like a kid, my hugeness taking up the whole room. I bounced again. "Hi, Daddy," I said. Maybe I was acting like a kid to remind him of how we used to be happy, a happy family. Don't leave your kids! Your babies! "Pops, you have a giant belly here." Straddling him, I patted him there and continued bouncing. "Are ya pregnant?"

He sort of roared, sat up, and batted me on the face again. "Get off," he said. Johnny was winding up.

On the bed, curled up and reaching toward him from where I'd fallen into the mattress, I felt like a zoo person, in the den with the giant wild aging mammoth-toothed bear.

I would take care of him, though, and made a mental note to look into the prerequisites for a career in zoology next time I was at the Volusia County Library.

"What the fuck?" he said. "What the fuck is this?"

"I want to kiss you," I said, whispering into the mattress. "Goodnight. I'm here to tuck you in. Do you need anything?"

I was a jellyfish against my father's soft sides. I did not move. My face burned like it was raw in the salty wind, and my tears were the giant wet balls kind. I pushed the tears out of my eyes as hard and fast as I could. I could feel my nose filling up, with pain, or wetness, or more crying.

I straddled him. I tried. I tried to get him to look me in the eye. My hands pressed on his cheeks. I pushed myself, my bone between my legs, onto his enormous bloated stomach. I was a tiny float on the ocean, a blue marker. My long new strong legs grasshoppered to my ears. I was a big bug, a smiling thing that blew in from the air. I felt dizzy, twenty-three floors up, mantising him. I cradled his cheeks. They scratched like muffins, poppyseed muffins in my hands—black dots and softness.

He'd gotten a beer—from under the pillows? From the nightstand? And I nearly jumped as high as the ceiling when he popped it open.

"Georgia, goddammit, get the fuck off me, I mean it. What is the problem here?"

I *was* off him, but I climbed back on. "Can I have a sip of your beer," I said. I'm not sure whom I was trying to get in trouble, him, me, or my mom. I felt like I was pretending to be Cheryl, the bad girl at my last school. She liked being bad and was not afraid of it.

"She's emotionally disturbed," my mother said, as if saying a difficult thing for the first time. I didn't hear her come in the room.

"Whoa!" I said, and I sprang off him, whirled around on the bed. He moaned and said please stop gyrating all about the place—it was making him sick.

"Be still," he said, his face tight, mean.

"Mom!" I wrapped up tight again in my sheets. The fabric was damp, sweaty. "Where's Sid?"

"What's going on?" Her hair was all sprung out of her head. She looked smart and sturdy and strong. She looked like a person who knows the future. Agh, I thought. I should have hypnotized her *first*!

"Go to your room," she said.

I put my hands on my breasts, a living bra, over my sheets. "I'm too old for that, Ma." It surprised me how afraid I was, but how easy it was to pretend. I simply said to myself, *don't care about anything.*

My mother said she and my father needed to talk, and I was to excuse myself. At once. "Go, scoot."

My father said talking was a goddamn foolish waste of time.

"Will you please watch your language?" she said, buzzing. "I will not be around language."

"You said you wanted to talk," he said. "I'm talking. I'm fucking talking, MC. THIS IS TALKING!" he screamed. He threw his beer can at the dresser, where it landed, sitting straight up.

"Quite the feat," I said. "Ha ha." I was walking past my mother, sashaying to beat the band.

Then I heard Sid out there thumping and banging and the chair tipping over, creaking as he grabbed the drapes to make it from the sofa to the recliner, him stepping on the glass coffee table to make it back to the sofa, which we were definitely not allowed to step on.

My whole hugeness slowly filled the room.

"Don't," my mother said. "Don't do it." She reached out and grabbed my arm, hard.

I wrenched it free. "I'll make you see me naked," I said. I thought perhaps I am pure evil, and this is what we do.

"What?" she said.

Then the door slammed shut. Now, who would take this seriously? Sid didn't even know where San Antonio was, or anyone there, except that girl from sixth grade, who swam with us that one cloudy day.

Then the door opened again, and I heard him lope down the hall, and suddenly, Sid was sidled against my mother. He kissed her on the cheek. She hugged herself and kept him away with her elbows and arms. I slid down onto the floor and hugged myself, too. Sid had on a jacket of my father's, a buckskin thing, with heavy white topstitching. The pockets bulged.

"It was nice knowing ya," Sid said to me. He sounded old and angelic. His lips sticky, his black hair shredded around his face. I thought of his hut on the beach, water swirling its floor, the hut not unlike Sid in shape, color, texture.

He left; we heard the front door slam the second time. My father asked us to please give him the peace he needed. "I need peace."

"Georgia," my mother said. She leaned against the mirrored, folding doors of the closet. "You have to decide."

I wanted to check on Sid—I wanted to run after him. He wouldn't leave. But I should go to him, maybe. My father's clock gave way to another moment, and he rolled onto his side. "Decide what?" I said. I didn't know what she was talking about.

"Okay," he muttered, and there was more muttering, and he talked himself back to sleep.

"Are you ready to assume the responsibilities of adulthood you seem so eager to take on, to rush into pell-mell?" My mother's eyebrows thrust themselves at me, dark arrows—pointing at me, two fierce *No*'s.

I jutted out my hip and, flouncing past her, said "Pell-*mell*?" I ran through the condo, pretending, in my sheets, that I was wealthy and distressed for good reason.

Dashing to the balcony, I leaned over and saw our wagon easing out of the parking lot and into the crazily busy late-night A1A traffic below.

"It can't be. But it is. Oh, no way," I said. "No way." I said, "Dear Lord, please return our little brother to us." I was trying to find a mood that fit. "You little bastard." That was it. I banged my palms on the railing. I wailed. I didn't know, at first, why I was so angry. Then it was so obvious. He didn't take me with him. He didn't even ask.

I ripped off my sheet and threw it over the balcony. It fluttered down, nothing like a parachute. My body broke out in goose bumps. I was a tan girl, but felt pasty white in the moonlight and neon. The sheet balled onto itself and slipped onto the Parker's balcony, two down and one over. It was out of sight in a second. "Ah," I said. I watched the wagon stop at a red light. How had this child learned to drive? What had I been doing?

Even naked, no one saw me. I covered my breasts.

I saw police lights flashing up at the corner, at the 7-Eleven; a car was pulled over at a crazy angle—a boy—-not Sid—stood at the pay phone, holding the phone in front of his belly.

Getting dressed, I thought *growth spurt—never again*. Pus seemed likely to spurt. Bile and oil and geysers. Early on, a girl got the idea the growth spurt everyone waited for wasn't going to be good. It's in fact going to be the worst thing.

And I was growing taller and more pointy *as I lived and breathed*. I walked back all tall and nightgowny and sweating hard, back down the hall and into their room. My dad lay back, watery and vague, blind, it seemed, on the bed. It just didn't look like this man could see anything. It was as though the world had become too wildly incomprehensible for him to keep seeing it.

My mother stood, frozen, by the mirrored closet doors, thousands of her reflected down a narrow scary hallway of infinite mirrors, tinier and tinier, all those mothers. I saw them, like attacking soldiers sneaking up on her. My mother, she was trying to stop time. She was trying to get us all to go back and take a different road.

"Everything's gone," she said flat and hard. "Daddy's wallet, the car keys—gone. What do you think about that? Are you happy? Are you getting what you want, little miss?"

"Mom," I said bitterly. I quickly thought of the car I saw, it was not *really* our car.

"Why didn't you stop him? Why don't you try?" She was talking to me, but looking at herself in the mirrors of mirrors in the hallway that led into the bedroom. There was my father, a breathing giant. She looked just as angry as she did when she saw me straddling my daddy. Like my being on top of him squirted my brother out into the night, pressed him into this deed. I was taking up too much space, her eyes said. I was developing into a problem girl.

"Okay," I said. "Fine." I flounced over, pecked my dad on the cheek in a mean way. "Your only son is gone, you know." I flicked past her, and I was saying, with my hips and breasts, *okay fine I'll be that way. I'll be the bad thing.*

In my mind, as I got into my bed, crying, my bedsheet was falling, falling, falling from our balcony, a fluttering white wave, dry, perfect, and dropping, softly. In my mind, that white, that wave—it never reached the ground.

In the Drink

$\mathbf{I}$t turned out she was riding her bike to the Rollins College campus every day, fifteen miles north of our house in Orlando. She was taking classes so she could apply to their law school.

"I want you to get a ten-speed, Mom," my brother said. I mocked him at the time he said it, but that night, falling asleep in our dark dusty house, the furniture still draped in white sheets, it occurred to me that Sid was the only person in our family with good ideas. At least when it came to transportation and safety.

I did not let on to him that I knew this, though. When Sid and I walked to school together, we argued.

"She's insane, she's crazy," I said. I slapped him on the head.

"He's the one who's an asshole," Sid said. He spit by my foot. And then on our first Friday back, at the bus stop, I leaned against the hedge, like usual, and watched for the other kids and the bus. Sid just kept on walking.

I continued to pretend he was not a boy with whom I was particularly acquainted.

He was a walking stick, down the shady oak-lined street.

"You're really strange," Debbie James said to me as the bus pulled up. She hadn't ever spoken to me before. She was a luminous blonde with my hair, only well behaved and smelling great. She had expensive clothes: sundresses, crocheted sweaters, and the first Walkman in our school. "I feel for you," she said, dripping.

I happened to know her mother was a terrible alcoholic and her father was gone, really gone, sailing around the world with rich people on yachts, some said. Others said he left with a high school girl, a girl from the Catholic school.

When she spoke to me, I looked at the ground and thought about her pale thin mother sprawled out on their lanai with a martini glass askew in her fingers, and I didn't say anything. When the bus arrived, I followed Debbie on as usual.

"I'm aboard; the world can start revolving again," Debbie said. She stopped, swiveled her body around, and sashayed to the back of the bus. The kids groaned. I pretended she was my friend as I followed her down the aisle.

We passed Sid as we turned onto Michigan Avenue. He was carrying two plastic bags, like water buckets, and running, like thieves in movies run, scooting across the parking lot of the grocery store like the land was on fire.

After dinner Sunday night, my father came in and announced that we were going to the block party.

"What block party?" I said. We followed him out into the driveway.

"Buck, you can't be serious." My mother leaned on the mailbox in our driveway. "All that water down there. You can't."

My dad said to her, "You are the most unhappy woman I have ever met."

He was sloshing his drink around, other hand on his hip, sideways to her, glowering. "Just come on with us. Live for once. Have a good time!" My father showed her his big mouth of teeth and hit himself on the side of the head. "It's not complex."

It was, though, and Sid and I knew it. Things were complex.

Our house wasn't being altogether paid for; my mother wanted us to keep our voices down, keep a low profile; we didn't really fit in this neighborhood (thank God for Oscar Love and his funky hippie mother, who lived in an odd bunker house, completely out of place among the swanky contemporary and Colonial houses). We had the right house, it seemed to me. We were simply the wrong family. If it weren't for Oscar Love, his weirdo truck-driving dad, the cement-block house with snake cactus growing all over it, we would have been the worst people on the whole street.

"There's no party, I'm telling you." Mom was pulling her hair back tight from her face. "It's Sunday," she whispered. "Who's going to be there?"

My father gave her a shove. A play shove, but she is small, and she took two steps back and threw her arms out into the air. She looked so tiny when he pushed her, like a pinwheel, like someone falling.

He turned and wove down the driveway, dancing and singing under the huge oaks with all that Spanish moss, in silver shiny curls like his hair. "Sometimes it's hard to love a woman," he sang, kind of a yodel, as he walked away from us. Then Sid ran after him, and then I did, too.

My mother called out in a perfect whisper-yell: "Don't swim. Don't go inside their house. Stay outside and come right back. Be very polite and thank the hostess and host. Remember your manners and don't touch anything."

"Let's festivate, people!" My father yelled into the dead silent night. He was loose up in the Partain's lawn. Sid and I walked the straightest line we could, behind him all the way. Now Sid followed me because he always did. He was my pet. A dark-haired wire-fur pet.

Between us and the Loves were the Sedleckys. Mr. Sedlecky, whom my father called Old Man Sedlecky, though they had never met, was head of garbage at Disney World. Theirs was a mansion, brick, with balconies and climbing bougainvillea and a wrought-iron fence of spears. That's where the party was.

Now my father was tap-dancing down the middle of our street, doing this *Fiddler on the Roof* dance he liked to do. I flicked my elbows and arms around, bonked Sid on the head, and looked away from my mother. When I headed down to the lake like this, I always thought I could see down past Kissimmee Way, to the spires of Cinderella's castle, but Sid said it was Mars I was seeing, and I knew in my heart's heart that spike of silver was another plain star. I knew in my heart there was a party, and I hoped in my stomach and my feet that we had been invited.

"It's a block party," my father shouted back up the quiet street. His enthusiasm always made me nervous and doubtful. I couldn't see my mother anymore. I caught up to him and grabbed his moist hand. He dropped mine and ruffled his curly permed hair, straightened his guyabera, and then opened it another two buttons. "The world is welcome to a fucking a block party!"

"Ya trying to be sexy, Pops?" Sid said.

"I am sexy," my dad said. "Hoody-hoo!"

He cut across the wide immaculate Sedlecky lawn. "Party time! Hooody-hoo!" he yelled, waving his arms, as though he were in charge of the night, of all fun. He danced down the Sedlecky driveway. I was afraid and hoping people were seeing him.

"Wait up, y'all," I said. Usually Sid stayed behind with my mother when my father ran off to do something fun. But Sid was right there, being all crazy with his arms, pretending to dance, too. Usually it was me who stayed right with Buck, went out with him on Sunday afternoons. We had danced the two-step in the craziest bars. I had learned the wild man dance, the chicken dance, and how to drink a shot. I was fourteen. I loved this father. No one like him.

I touched my skin. It was sweaty, just as I suspected. I was wearing green shorts, a striped orange shirt, a boy's shirt, and "barefoot sandals," plastic soles with shoelaces that laced between your toes and up your ankles any way you wanted; Cleopatra of the schoolyard, that's who I was. I was thinking maybe my dad was right. We could be having a lot more fun in this family if my mother wasn't such a wet blanket. He wasn't so crazy. It was a party. We were fun people; we weren't that weird of a family.

"Oscar will be there," I said to my dad. Oscar was sixteen but in my class at school. He was in the wrong grade because he'd been educated experimentally in his younger years; those years hadn't counted. People didn't like him. Oscar read philosophy, never combed his dark patches of hair, and he dressed in flowered pants and striped shirts. Making him, I thought, the perfect husband for me.

Oscar Love. He was the main reason I left my mother in the driveway with her hands, caught like birds, in her hair. Oscar Love. He was the reason I was keeping my parents together, being nice to them, helping them calm down whenever I could. I wanted to be married off to Oscar in a nice wedding.

It wasn't even like a real name, it was made-up sounding, like a senator or a cartoon boy. It was a command. It was a door, and I was walking through it.

Georgia Love. Sounded more like a star, a sexy star. A hick name was *Georgia Jackson*. It really didn't suit me at all. My mother thought it was such an elegant name. I couldn't wait to get rid of it. As soon as my boobs were all there, I was going to start feeling a lot more like Georgia Love. I grinned thinking about it and shadowed my father down the steps, around to the pool.

Now that I was fourteen, I was starting to think seriously about getting married, and I needed to think about making love; I didn't have the leeway to act like a kid anymore. Everything seemed to matter. Every encounter with Oscar might matter, might move me closer to the wedding, me, like Stevie Nicks, floating across the water, in the sunset, our matching motorcycles waiting onshore.

"Goddamnit!" my father said. He was checking his shoes, his soles.

"You stepped in it," Sid said. They weren't even trying to be quiet. As I caught up I smelled it.

"Go back," I said. "Change your shoes. We can wait here. We will wait for you."

"Wait at the party," Sid said. "We could wait there."

"Goddamnit to hell, for Jesus' sake. Goddamnit! Your mother puts these curses on me, the woman is a witch, she's a goddamn witch!" He yanked off his expensive dress shoe and flung it into the Prentisses' hedge. Sid ran for it.

I peeked around the corner and saw candles floating in the pool, but no people.

"I saw where it landed!" Sid shouted. I stood there at the side of the house with my arms hugging myself, hoping no one could see. Lights flicked on in the dark low house across the lake. Then, a couple—she was in a white dress, and he was in a business suit—came out of the shadows, greeted us, and swiftly walked past, as though they had been down these stairs plenty of times. They were gliding kind of people. Not my favorites, that kind.

"We're fine," I said, but they were already around the corner.

My father yanked off the other shoe and then his socks.

"Don't want to ruin a perfectly good pair of socks," he said. He balled them and put them in his pocket, and he bulged out in an odd way.

"I've got it!" Sid said, and he backed up out of the shrubs like a little efficient truck. He had his red towel wrapped around his shoulders, looking like a practice Batman, so cute, I couldn't believe it. He brought the shoe to my dad. My dad didn't thank him. He flung the shoe Sid'd carefully brought onto the roof of the Prentisses. A string of lights in their yard clicked on.

Then my dad flung the other one. "Serenade to the flying zapatos!" he sang out, and their garage security lights buzzed on.

"Oh, man," Sid whispered.

"Daddy," I said. "Well, it's okay if you are barefoot since it is an outdoor function, right?"

I thought I could still make out my mom, way up at the end of the street, leaning by the mailbox, stiff with sadness and fear. In my mind's eye. I could feel her.

Then my father patted himself down, wiggled his toes, which were white as grubs in the moonlight. We went, arm in arm, down the steps, the three of us.

"I hope people are wearing suits," Sid said.

I said I was sure they would not be.

"My children, my beautiful children," Dad whispered. I couldn't think what he had done with his glass.

But soon he had another one, and more to hold.

The Sedleckys had placed a life-size blow-up Mickey Mouse on the diving board. Mickey stood there, swaying in the evening breeze. My father barreled across the patio. Behind Mickey was a tray table, with glasses filled to the brim. Sid and I stuck close to his body. Like you maybe do with a sinking ship.

There were clusters of couples—dressed up, in summer gowns and summer seersucker suits—all over the patio.

"Oh, that's *fab*, Barbie," I heard a woman say, in a laughing voice. Was she being serious, or was she pretending to be at a party, a dopey party. I looked around for Oscar as my dad trotted from group to group, looking for one that would welcome him in.

"I want you to meet my friends," he said.

"No, no, no, we don't want to," Sid said. Sid wanted to go home. No one was wearing a bathing suit. His lips were compressed. Two years ago, he would have cried, but he was twelve now and only cried in the garage.

Music tinkled out over the pool. The pool was part of a deck that ramparted over the lake. On the other side of the lake, Orlando glittered gold and blue; the sky was a tiny bit pink on the edges; Disney sat beyond.

I took a deep breath—my father was leaning *way* over the water, grabbing the Mickey, trying to grab its bottom and pull it over to him. Mickey kept bobbing out of reach.

"Dad! Look out! You're going to fall in!" Sid sounded furious.

My father snagged the Mickey and was doing a salacious dance with him on the patio, pressing the Mickey against him. Sid was sitting on the lip that ran around the inside of the pool, churning his legs so that the candles traversed, hard enough to make things move. He churned, didn't splash. The Partains and the Prentisses slid away from the pool, their groups moving, intact, like in a game or a dance. The tinkling music was playing, and I noticed there were no other kids here, when someone tapped me on the shoulder.

"Hoody-hoo!" my dad yelled. It would have been funny, but more at a kid's party, maybe. Dancing with the Mouse like that.

I turned then, away from Sid and my dad, to see who was tapping me. I'm visiting, I could say. I could say I was an au pair from France.

"Hey," Oscar said. He was in a dashiki and wide paisley pants—the picture of elegance and charm.

"Oh," I said. "You're here. Were you invited?" I tried to block my father from Oscar's view, but Oscar was a foot taller than me, in platform boots. I could feel that Mickey bobbling with my father on the deck.

"Sure," he said. He stared into my pupils. He spoke slowly. "Sure," he said.

"Just asking," I said.

"Wouldn't miss it," he said. "Ruby's here." He pointed over to where his mother talked with four men; Ruby's finger poked out, into the group of men. She lectured them, her red hair and red dress dull and somehow earthy-serious. Her leather earrings looked like paddles hanging off her ears. "So if you want to talk trade, if you want to talk about that kind of thing, bucko, that's what I'm saying." Her voice struck across the patio, the water, hard and heavy. I watched Oscar's face to see if this loud mother bothered him. He was smiling and peering up at the sky as though it were a ceiling, something close.

He lived with her. The two of them, in the weird bunker. Oscar's dad was a trucker, and Oscar always said, "My dad, he's over the road."

A port-wine stain covered Oscar's right cheek, and a bit of his forehead. The stain was the shape of Florida, the panhandle, the darkest wine, across his forehead. The body of the state, its edges almost raised looking, appeared outlined, pasted on. I had spent hours memorizing the contours of Oscar's stain in class over the years. Orlando was below his eye; our life together could disappear when he smiled or grimaced. Sadly, his regular pimple appeared as Sanford, not an important Florida city. There was also no Lake Okeechobee. I was surprised I was noticing the stain tonight at all; I hadn't in a long time. I think it was because I was about to pretend, about to be, someone else, and so he seemed like a stranger to me, too.

"So," he said, and he rocked back on his heels.

"Yes," I said. "So." I looked up at the sky, wishing I knew the name or location of something, anything.

"So." He shifted his weight and took a drink of his beer. At sixteen, Oscar had that smell of sweat and boy and hair—the way I figured a bear probably smelled. "What's up, Georgia," he said.

"Oh. You know. I don't know." I grinned, showing my teeth in the new way I had been practicing.

"George," Sid said. "Let's go." Dripping, loudly, he tugged on my hair. Sharply, I yanked on his red towel cape. Groups of people, holding plastic Mickey Mouse plates and cheese, murmured.

"Go swim," I said.

"Take a long walk off a short dock," Oscar said, but he rubbed his palm across Sid's spiky hair and noogied him with his fist. Sid's bony cheek seemed to love Oscar's grinding fist.

Sid said, "We're not swimming; there're candles in there. Of all the idiot ideas."

"Sid," I said. "We just got here. We're having fun!"

"I'm gonna go home," Sid said.

"No, Oscar, tell him he has to stay," I said.

"Hey, he's free," Oscar said. "Little dude, your choice, man."

I heard my father calling out to his friends, "Hey, Judge! Hey, Tits!"

Sid knew he couldn't leave. He couldn't leave.

"Hey, bro," Oscar said. "I'll give you five dollars if you go get me and the Missus drinks."

"The *Missus*?" Sid poked his whole fist in his mouth and made a retching noise. Sid took the fiver.

"Judge, Judge," my father yelled at a man walking in through sliding glass doors. "Judge!" I let my father steer me into the Sedleckys' Florida room.

"I want you kids to meet Judge England. He is the most important judge in the state of Florida, and a good old boy. Now come on." My father had his wet hands on my shoulders, a drink on my right shoulder. I wanted my father to do a good job. I wanted to help him make a good impression. I was afraid if I left him, and went back to Oscar, my father would fall on his face.

Judge England was draped with a tall treelike blonde woman in high silver sandals. The hem of her dress fluttered unevenly, like butterfly wings, melty colors. I didn't look up. The Judge hadn't stopped talking to a man—I think it was Mr. Colby, because he was wearing a silky purple shirt, and Mr. Colby was a disco guy—but my father, like a crazy dog, kept bobbing, trying to get in.

"Oh. Children." The blonde draped woman said, "I love children." She talked like she had acorns in her mouth. Behind her, out the doors, the pool shone like a mean mirror.

"Hello, Mim," my father said. "Don't tell me you're still ticked off."

"The ragamuffin?" The Judge drained his drink and excused himself. It's like they were talking in code. The Judge disappeared.

"Buck Jackson, you are scaring my action away," the woman said. "Let's go outside where we can hear."

"I can hear fine," I said.

"You must be Georgia Jackson. How is your mother, dear?" But they were walking away, my father with his arm around this Mim's waist, and that turned out to be a good thing because I had no idea how to tell this woman how my mother was. How *was* my mother? It seemed a very strange question to me, and that made me feel so ridiculously bare of brain, I tripped and hit my father's back hard, saving myself.

"What?" My father nearly toppled in the pool. Then he turned, sharp on his bare heels, got new bearings altogether, pointed himself to the giant brightly lit house all opened up, and he faced it, spreading his arms wide. "Kids, get over here. Embrace the evening!" But we were already right by him, Sid too, proffering tall pink drinks.

My dad didn't seem to notice this; he threw his arms back, leaned back from his waist, and beat his chest, Tarzaning out a huge whoop.

"So what do you want to be when you grow up?" the drapey woman asked Sid in her crepe-paper voice.

"Buried at sea," Sid said. She looked at him like she hated him. Like he was a gnat and she hated him.

"Daddy," I said, and tapped his shoulder. "We should go."

"Okay," he said, flicking the butt into the sky. "All right. There. Where was I." He moved from me fast, broke into a dance. His thin black pants made his legs like licorice, shiny and stretchy. He danced back into the house, a barefoot jig.

Sid had brought me a virgin drink, he said. "It's a club soda with a lime."

It had a Minnie Mouse stirrer. "Yeah, get some more of these," I whispered at him.

He whispered to me, "I'm going to be a millionaire."

"You Jackson kids," Oscar's mom said. "Look at your dad. He's the life of the party, huh!"

I turned and looked. Buck was tangoing with that Mim woman. "Where's your mom?" Ruby looked hot and sweaty, like she'd been playing a sport. Her body was all freckled, and she smelled like grass. She wasn't drinking anything. She stood there, barefoot, fiddling with her turquoise rings, smart and awake. "Didn't she come down?"

"Hiding," Sid said.

"Oh," Ruby said.

"Sid," I said.

"Georgia's in love with Oscar," Sid said.

I whacked him, and Ruby smiled at us both, as though we were very tiny and very unrealistic.

Then two loud-talking men came up to Ruby and said they had the proof and she may as well give up.

"Okay, y'all," she said. "You want to go inside and sit down and really talk?" She sounded tough and sure of herself.

Oscar was standing behind her, his feet wide apart, kind of lording over her, but she didn't seem to mind, even though she sure didn't need him horning in, anyone could see that. With Oscar behind her, they looked like man and wife—he a twenty-five-year-old-looking sixteen-year-old, and she a twenty-five-year-old-looking thirty-five-year-old.

"Eat 'em up, Ruby," Oscar said, and he sent her off with the wheeler-dealers.

"What are they talking about," I said flatly. I didn't want to sound interested.

"She writes about you in her diary *all* the time," Sid said.

I took a long, noisy final suck on my party drink and pretended to empty the contents over Sid's head. Then I started chewing on the Minnie Mouse stirrer, trying to make more eye contact with Oscar.

My father began to sing "When a Man Loves a Woman," loudly.

"Uh," Sid said quietly, "I'm out of here."

If I could get Oscar down to the beach, we could start talking, and I could tell him interesting things. Maybe we could kiss.

I didn't see where Sid went. Oscar walked down the stairs to the beach by himself. Ruby steered the two businessmen alongside the pool, a hand planted on the back of each one's suitcoat. There, my father danced astride the tiled edge, leaning back, singing, looking happy. I don't think Ruby saw him, because she was behind the two men. Ruby was a very petite woman.

My dad and now Mim were swaying on the lip, maybe they thought they were dancing. Mim Satterwhite was my mother's least favorite person. The Satterwhites lived behind us, in Jewel Hills, which wasn't as nice as Jewel Oakes, where we lived. My mother hated Mim Satterwhite because she cavorted about her Florida room, watering her plants in the nude.

Tonight Mim wore a long filmy flowered dress, a plastic hibiscus in her hair, and blue eye shadow. Her silver lamé heels slipped along the edges of the pool. They were getting ruined. Her face was always *surprised*! or *excited*! Her lips were fish lips, moving with her from one emotion to the next. She and my father careened down toward the diving board, and now made their way back toward me. I was standing alone on the patio, chewing on my stirrer.

"There's some top-notch livestock here tonight," my dad said over Mim's shoulder, to me.

"Dad," I said. I wanted to die.

Buck chose that moment to pirouette Mim, and then he looped Mim's rubbery arms up and about, so that he could be pirouetted, too. I took two long steps over, one at a time, like you do in Mother May I.

Ruby spun around, Mim shrieked, and my father, teetering over the edge, grabbed at the air, which was filled with the short fat guy's suitcoat tails. Ruby stuck her arms out to my dad, and so did I, but neither of us was close enough.

I saw what that guy did. He pushed my father. Harder than necessary. It was true he was losing his balance. It was true the other guy was pushing *off* my father so he wouldn't fall in the pool, the pool with all those candles in it.

"Hey, hey, hey, hey, hey," Ruby barked out.

No one heard me; I said, "He can't swim." Which was true. My father couldn't swim.

But the man pushed my father, and my father sloped down into the water in slow motion, and he took Mim Satterwhite screaming down with him into the water. A slow wake plowed away from them, snuffing the tea candles in a fell swoop.

"Oh man, oh man," I said, and I hopped to the side of the pool and knelt down, extending my arm toward the flopping disaster that was my father and Mim.

The host appeared behind Ruby and said, "Do we have a problem?"

"Do you have a lifeline?" she said. She was twisting her scarf, about to cast it toward the drowners.

My father's guyabera took in air, made a big bubble on his back, and then he went under.

"He's going to hit his head," I said. Which he did on the wall as he banked down, down, down into the deep end, and I thought he was dead. Mim was pressing on him, in order to keep her own head up; my mother was right about that woman. I screamed "Oscar!" but Oscar was already there. I was about to jump in.

"Oh my God," I cried. My father was sinking to the bottom, and he had never let go of Mim Satterwhite's left hand. She was all draped down in with him, her leg on the lip, her dress bleeding green and red and blue into the water. Mostly, Mim seemed to be trying not to get her hair wet. My dad held Mim's hand with both of his, below her, his body listing like a wreck. He kept yanking her down, which would have been funny to watch if he'd had gills or something.

"I'm calling 911," Mr. Sedlecky said.

"You should, my gosh in heaven," a woman said.

"How did they fall in?"

"Tipsy-dipsy!" someone said in a mean laughing voice. The party had congregated on the patio behind us.

Oscar dove in, fully clothed. Sid dove in after, flinging off his cape behind him. I couldn't believe I wasn't rescuing anyone. Ruby grabbed the long buoy and the pole with the hook—the safety equipment you had to have. She threw them both into the water, as Oscar brought my dad up.

"Hoo-boy," my dad yelled, and he raised his fist in a cheer.

"I'm saying, everybody, jump on in! Pool party!" Mim yelled.

"She walked in with a drink," I heard Mrs. Madigan say. Mrs. Madigan had been the state cheerleading champion. I liked her, until she said that.

"Okay, there we go," Ruby said. "You got it, boys." She was nodding at Oscar, who was scooping my father up the stairs. Oscar steered my dad with one hand. My dad lay back into Oscar, as though Oscar were a folding chair. "Ah, my billfold," Oscar said, and he tossed it at my feet. I felt very helpful suddenly. I picked it up. Sid was frog-kicking behind Mim, easing her to the steps. My father snorted like a dog, shaking his head. "My glasses," he said.

"Got 'em," Oscar said. "We got everything here, Buckeroo."

"Oh my god, we've gone boomsie boom!" Mim Satterwhite said. "And me here all exposed, my dress is totally see-through. Look, you can see everything." She stood on the steps and turned slowly, modeling for us. Sid was wiping off with a towel, and I skipped over and asked him if he was okay.

"As much as one can be. Can you believe that woman?" Sid, pert and sparkly, let me wipe his hair and his back. I tried to be rough with him. We watched Oscar get my father patted down.

"Oh, Lawsy," Mim kept squealing. "I'm bra-less. I'm so risqué!"

"Is someone getting her a towel or something?" Mrs. Madigan said.

"This is ridiculous, ridiculous," Mr. Sedlecky said. "Come on, people."

My father collapsed at my feet, sitting all wonky, like a kid with bad legs. Then he barfed up an enormous pool of water and set to coughing.

"Hoo-yah!" he said, and he tried to sit up. "Gawd," he said. "Where'd that come from?"

"Are you okay?" I said, bending to him.

"I think he'll live," Oscar said.

"I think he will live," Sid said. I knelt down beside my dad and brushed his hair off his cool face.

"Get off me," he said. He was patting himself all over, clumsily. I jumped back from him. I felt like he'd bitten me.

The tea lights had all sailed down to the shallow end and hovered there, unlit, like bad ideas.

"My goddamn wallet," he said. He lay back on the patio and closed his eyes. He looked like a huge frog, grounded on its back.

I wanted to fall in, I wanted to save him, but I couldn't do it. If he had died, I would have been nearly an orphan. I could have moved in maybe with Oscar and Ruby; my mother would be stricken and go to the Sunnyland mental institution if my father died in a pool at a party with people watching.

No one was paying attention to Mim. I ambled around on the deck, trying to figure out what to do with myself. I wanted to be asked to go for a walk. I wanted to be asked anything at all by Oscar. Sid came toward me, but I waved him away. He shrugged and put on the Mickey Mouse shirt Sedlecky had thrown at him.

Mim was holding her hair, with both hands, and it was taking her a long time to get up the stairs and onto the deck. Finally, she made it out of the water. She took off her heels and began to ring out her dress, her legs splayed wide. A swirl of colors circled behind her in the pool. Her dress dripped purplish red. Her mascara was running down both sides of her face. It was a frightening sight.

"Buck, honey, you are right here, just reach for my arm," Ruby said. My father sputtered. As he got to his feet, Mim stumbled past him, and I saw him reach up and squeeze her butt, the right side, the fabric of her dress mashing and wrinkling under his pressure. *I did not see that,* I thought. But I saw Ruby seeing it too. Her lips compressed, her eyes opened wider. She tilted her chin down to her neck. I mimicked this, to see how it would feel. It didn't feel like anything. Probably, Mim didn't even notice that Buck did that. Probably Ruby had seen a lot of stuff like that. It wasn't a big hairy deal.

I looked around to see if there was anything else I could do, any other person I could attach myself to. Anything but going home with him.

Oscar disappeared. Sid was in the process of disappearing—I saw his legs flopping over the sea wall—he had dropped himself down onto the beach.

Oh, I thought, *I am going to be an old maid with a sick father. I am going to be like a girl in a book. Not a real girl.*

Sirens droned, closer.

"Goddamnit, people," Sedlecky said. "Okay, are we okay here?"

"Yes, I'll get him home, y'all. I think we're fine. Can you take her?"

"What about the sirens," I said, worried we had summoned the authorities for nothing.

"I'll take care of it, it's really a nonissue." Sedlecky opened the gate, way in advance of our reaching it, and the three of us, Ruby and Dad and me, tracked out to her car, on the street.

"Well," my father said, coughing. He broke loose of Ruby. "That was refreshing!" He twirled. "Yes, quite refreshing."

"At least you had already thrown off your shoes, Pop," I said. I carried his shoes, two damp boats, one in each hand.

"You weren't much help, you know," my father said, and he whacked me across the back of the legs. In front of Ruby.

"I seem to have left my drink down at the bottom somehow," Buck said.

"Oh, nothing he hasn't seen before!" Mim said, her voice carrying over the house, across the lawn.

Ruby said, "Let's get you home, Buck Jackson," she said. My father was bleary and blinking and helpless-looking, patting himself down. "I don't think I was wearing my paperwork," he said.

I stuck close to Ruby. "Should we try to locate Oscar, do you think?" I said. I knew it was dumb to say this, but I couldn't help it. Something made me say his name out loud as frequently as possible. As though if I kept saying it, he would become closer to me, and then mine.

"Sit here, Buck Jackson and behave yourself," she said. She popped the locks, and Buck got in the back, and I sat up front with her.

We walked across our driveway. My mother's bedroom lights flicked on, then the hallway ones, then the foyer.

"My shoes are out here somewhere," Buck said. He stood in the lawn.

"Well, we will just enjoy the suspense of that," Ruby said.

"My dad's taking us to Disney," I finally said. Ruby smiled in the dark, and my mother came out, and I dropped Ruby's hand. "Maybe we could visit the leather stall then," I said.

"Where the hell is the boy?" my father said.

"What in God's name," my mother said, running.

"Oscar's with him. They're fine," Ruby said to my mother. I don't think she realized my mother was wigged out at the sight of my soaked father.

My father looked at her, his eyes watery but alive, focusing on Ruby like a fish, with interest—her body—swimming him toward her. He drifted to her.

"I knew this would happen," Mom said. She was in my dad's burgundy terrycloth robe and her old slippers, her hair set in pink curlers. Her face glistened with cold cream. "I knew this would happen, I knew it. Oh, Buck."

"Which thing, Mom?" I said. "What did you know?" It was partly curiosity, partly an accusation. I wanted her to throw her arms around Buck and invite Ruby and me in for cocoa. I was afraid she was making Dad feel terrible. And Ruby, too. My mom was ignoring her completely. And me! I realized I was furious at her. I wanted to shake her. I clasped my hands behind my back.

"So, Ruby Red, I owe you a drink, probably a whole dinner, for saving my life and all that," my father boomed. "Friday any good?" A light came on next door at the Ashington-Pickets. Buck shook his head like a golden retriever, and water flew all over my mom.

Ruby took his hand in her two hands, and I saw her ruby sparkling in the night. My father looked horrific, his pants clinging to his legs, the shirt like a hankie draped on him, his hair a matted wiglike thing. He was still dripping.

"It's been really nice getting to know all of you a little better," Ruby whispered, squeezing his hand. "Take it easy now. *Take it easy,* okay. Okay, everybody? Just kind of take it easy?" She smiled firmly. She took swingy steps backward to her car.

"Good-bye, Georgia," she said to me. "Be sweet now, honeybun. Good night, Mrs. Jackson," she said, smiling nicely and firmly, a small contained smile, to my mom. She closed the door with a quiet click and rolled the windows up tightly, sealing herself off from us, abandoning me to them.

Then she pulled out of the driveway in one long smooth motion and disappeared down to her house.

"What in heaven's name has happened," my mother said, whispering. The front door stood wide open. I could see moths in the light, flying into our house.

"Well, there did turn out to be a party," I said. "A lot of people there," I added. I stood on one foot then and stretched the other way out in front of me, flexing. "We wished you would have come."

"You can't do this," she said. She wasn't even listening to me.

My dad said he was going in to get some clothes on. "Perhaps pajamas," he said. "It's getting to be the pajama hour, I believe." He drifted to the house, but she intercepted him. *Like a jackal in the night,* I thought.

She blocked my father's way. She body-blocked him. "Just a minute, buster. Just what do you think you are doing!" She had her arms crossed, her legs spread wide, and when he tried to get around her, she hopped and planted herself in front of him. He whipped off his shirt, started twisting it, and then slapped her hard across the legs. It was like he wanted to play.

"You don't know what you've gotten yourself into," she said, louder. Lights came on at the Underwoods.

"Goddamnit, woman, we had a little fun. You could have come along," Dad said.

"Don't talk to me like that."

"Fuck you," he said. He threw his shirt down.

She stepped on it and stood in front of him again, like a soldier. "I won't stand for this. I won't."

"Hon," he said, yawning hugely.

"Hey," I said. "We could look for Sid." I figured he was with Oscar. I was thinking diversion: marry Oscar, kissing him all night long, what that would be like. Would he put his tongue in my mouth? Or just next to it.

I was pointing down the street, about to launch into my theory of where the boys had gone to, and why it was important we not let them get away with this, when my father gave my mother such a hard push that it sent her up against the croton bushes. She cried out, clamped her hand over her mouth, and grabbed the mailbox. I saw Mr. Underwood peek out of their side door, and then he popped back in, closed it quietly.

"Okay," she said. "Okay. That's how you want to play. That's how you want to play, Buck Jackson? This is who you are?" She was fierce, white-hot, breathing fire.

"Can I ask a question," I said in a loud, strong voice. I ripped off a huge chunk of my pinky fingernail and planted it in my mouth. "Because I really want to know, you know?"

"Get in the house," my father said. "Now."

"You are nothing to me," she said to him. "You're nothing. I don't feel anything." She was whispering. But I heard her. I heard.

I heard every breath.

Sinking

For ninth grade I got the most desirable teacher at Cherokee Indians School for the Gifted and Talented (formerly Sunshine School for Retarded Children) and the only man. Mr. Groover. Mr. Groover's specialty was cinnamon rolls and hands-on science.

I wanted to marry him. I knew I would.

Debbie made fun of him. Carol Dean Moldenhauer, Miss Perfect, made fun of him. He's so *femme*, they said. He's swish.

"Now they're *handicapped*," my mother said. "Now they're in classes. This is for the birds."

"Mom," I said, surprised. She'd been stressing compassion. "What's wrong with you?"

"With me? Nothing!"

"It's embarrassing for everyone involved, but hey, for them too, right?" Sid said. He was selling candy every morning on the front steps of the school—his own operation—and he gave the Sunshine kids a discount.

Three schools in one year. We'd left Holy Comforter because my mother had a falling out with the priest. It was a fascinating mystery; the idea of my strict mother fighting with a priest—I loved and loathed it. "That man is banned from our premises," she hissed. I'd never seen Father John at our house, but it sure was exciting to have a ban on someone. Then, Memorial Junior High closed after we'd been there a month because the new highway to Disney was going through it, right through the gym, literally, and that's how we ended up back downtown, at the converted retard school, which we shared with the Sunshine kids.

"But really, Mom. It doesn't make a lick of difference," Sid said. "School is school is school—who cares? The retards are cool."

I wasn't so sure. I noticed I didn't have friends. I noticed no one knew my name. I knew their names, every last one. I mean, it's not like I had anything to do but listen carefully to roll. "Mom," I said. "When am I allowed to start dating?"

She looked at me like I had just asked for the symptoms of polio. "What?"

"She's in love with Jere Groov-air." Sid flicked his wrist and talked with a lispy voice.

"What's wrong with that?" I said. I should have brought my *Science Today* book home, to study. I always forgot. Marie Curie didn't forget.

"Eighteen. You can be eighteen." We were eating dinner, and she gestured for me to pass her the butter.

"That's when we have to move out of the house you said." I held the butter just out of reach.

"It works out perfectly," she said, and she cleared her place at the table, abruptly.

I called out to her as she disappeared down the hall to her bedroom. "I'm asking Dad when he gets back."

"There's a good one," my mother yelled back, angry. "That's brilliant! Ask your father, Georgia!"

Sid reached his arm over to me. "Don't torment her totally," he said to me. "A little, yeah."

"I'm almost fifteen," I yelled. I didn't really want to yell. It didn't seem like what you do when you are fifteen. But something was making me yell. "Everyone in my school dates, why can't I?"

"Oh, God," Sid moaned, and he put his head down, right on his plate.

Mr. Groover brought his cinnamon rolls to us every Friday, steaming hot from his car. We imagined he picked them up at some sophisticated gleaming bakery in Winter Park, where he lived, and they rose and baked in the hot car on the highway while he commuted to downtown Orlando, and us, his ninth graders. Because we had the only male teacher in the school, we knew we were smarter and indulged and having fun.

On Fridays, he zipped around corners—we could see him walking down the open corridors of Cherokee Indians Junior High/Sunshine School, gliding smoothly and too gracefully, like a ballet dancer. He floated down the pink cement open-air halls of the school, past each grade. Mr. Groover was a butterfly with a gift. I could see myself in his arms in the place of the tray of cinnamon rolls.

With the metal tray of steaming cinnamon rolls outstretched on his arms, he didn't smile or frown as he came toward us. The boys in my class made fun of his hips, the way they swung around. He walked quickly. Yet everything about Mr. Groover was low-key, neat, tucked, suave, and calm. In his crisp black pants and fine white shirt (my mother had taught me to look at how far apart the stitches were on things, the closer the better), he looked like a waiter at a fancy restaurant. He had short brown hair, kind, bright brown eyes, a short organized beard, and a way of walking light on his toes that I liked to imitate.

"He is a total fag," they said.

"He takes it up the butt."

"The bare baloney, oh, man."

Andrew Hussman said, "El cornholio, el bungholio."

"Here comes the fag," John Trumble sang to the tune of "Here Comes the Bride."

"Limp wrist," Martin said, and he got up from his table and swished across the room, waving his wrist like Mr. Groover. A wrist? What was in a wrist that could be so awful? "Oh, oh, I need a dick to suck, pleath," Martin hissed. "Can I suck yours?" He was right in my face.

I didn't really know what he was talking about. But I didn't let on. "What's a condom?" John Trumble asked me every morning when I got to the merry-go-round, where we sat and kicked around, pretending, I guess, we were little kids, until it was time to go in for assembly. I gave Trumble my "I know but I am not saying" look, at least I hoped I did. That look involved me making my eyes big, and I had the tiniest eyes, blue fish eyes; I hated them. I knew I would think of the meanings, the strange meanings of these awful words; I always did.

I knew it would all come clear.

"Go away, John," I said.

"Good morning, my darlings! How are we doing today, this bright fine October Florida day?" Mr. Groover's words went up, up, up, up. He adored us.

Everyone laughed. I didn't. They were laughing when he came in the room, with our treats. Even Carol Dean Moldenhauer, whose father was a minister—the straightest girl in the school, Miss Perfect. Her mouth was a big rectangle—that's how she laughed, opening up and silently letting out something large and square from inside her. You could see her thick gums. She was class president, and she always wore green. She was slick. She turned her big laugh into a cheery "Good Morning, Mr. Groover," just as he entered his classroom.

"Good morning, boys and girls," Mr. Groover said. He looked like Mr. Rogers. "Good morning, Moldy."

It made my stomach hurt, those awful things the class said about our teacher, my future husband. Mr. Groover, he wasn't this thing they said he was, whatever it was, he was not bad. He was good.

"Oh, my God, y'all, sit!" Gail Cowert hissed at us. She was not my best friend, but I didn't mind her like some of the kids did. She was poor and her feet were dirty; you could see that because she only wore flip-flops, little green rubber 39-cent shoes. She'd gotten lice every year. She had moles, too, which somehow seemed related to her father's income, and her mother never made her wash her hair, so it was in thick strings, in her face, which was also oily. She was in Gifted and Talented because, they said, the PE teacher in Regular Track had tried to attack her. Attack Gail? I did not know.

After we ate our cinnamon rolls, Mr. Groover gave us wipettes, like you get at a restaurant. He used these on his camping trips, he said. He was a spelunker. Wipettes, he said, were one of the greatest inventions mankind knew. Did we not thank heaven for wipettes?

I did, to myself.

Sometimes he brought in maps and photos of caves he'd been in, in Kentucky and North Florida. People got married in the Bridal Tomb and in front of Wedding Bells, formations that dripped white pearls. That would be good, I always thought, for me and Mr. Groover. Georgia Groover. I wrote it down all the time, in fancy letters with roses entwined, and then when I was done, I turned the whole thing into roses on a trellis. But everyone was in love. Gail had a crush on John Trumble. Cynthia had a crush on my brother, of all people. John loved Staci Washington, who was going to Junior Miss pageants, even though no one we knew thought she was pretty; evidently, she was.

"Do you really spray hairspray on your butt to keep your underwear from creeping into your crack?" John'd ask Staci in front of anyone. I don't know what she saw in him.

Today Mr. Groover said we had a special opportunity, and Mr. Groover's special opportunities were usually guests and were always fabulous, like lion tamers, morticians, and stockbrokers. Somehow, they tied in to Science.

"I have a challenge for you this morning, class," he said. "We have talked a lot about spelunking, we know the difference between stalagmites and stalactites, and I've told you all about the Lemon Squeezer, and how to breathe in tight places, right class?" Mr. Groover, leaning on his desk, picked up a hanger, a kid's clothes hanger. "We know how to light a fire with wet wood. Please tell me we remember how to light a fire with wet wood. We've learned so much about sinkholes, Karst topography, and forest succession—I think this has been our best unit."

He bent the hanger into a circle. He was breathing and sucking in his ribs, stomach, everything. I imitated him in my seat. I put my hands on the notches of my waist.

Cynthia screamed that she was going to do it. I sat perfectly still. I was entirely happy at school and never wished it to end. I didn't talk because I didn't want to use up time.

Mr. Groover motioned Cynthia down and said, "Who is feeling slim and slender today? We're doing a little caving test here. To see who could actually make it!"

Mr. Groover demonstrated, and we couldn't believe. He slipped the hanger, the wire circle of it, down over his body, wiggling like licorice to get through.

Cynthia asked him if he'd been dieting.

"Bill and I have been caving in Kentucky," Mr. Groover said. He was pert.

John asked him if he had a kidney failure problem.

"What?" Andrew said. "You are such a geek, Trumble! That makes no sense at all."

Mr. Groover was asked to do it again, and he did, he slid it down his body like he was frisking himself, only faster; it was like magic, like that circle had no back. He did it the other way, slipping his point-tip wing tips into the ring in a deft hop, and drawing the circle up around his body, wriggling his hips, caving his chest, tucking his head, and voilà, he was free again. We laughed and laughed.

We'll have six kids, I decided. I thought we could name them after our favorite states. Florida, for sure. Alabama, and call her Allie.

Everyone wanted to try the spelunker test. John Trumble went foot first and pretended he couldn't get it over his hips. "I'm hung like a horse," he said.

Then he broke the hanger over his chest, and Mr. Groover unsnagged him from it and sent him back to his seat; he sat on his desk, and he said in his loud hoarse voice, "Georgia Jackson is Boney Maroni, skinny as a sticka macaroni, make her do it," and I turned red and got hot and slunk into my desk, and the Denson brothers said they could, they had to do this in football. The Denson brothers were huge.

Mr. Groover asked me to come up, but I had my head down on my desk; it was hard to move. Everyone was looking at me. He was talking to me. He never talked to me because I was good, perfect, and he never needed to. I felt he could read my mind, about the marriage, and I couldn't get up out of my seat.

Everyone tried but no one could do it, not one person. Finally Gail Cowert and I had to go because no one could get through without unsnapping the crinkle-tie at the neck of the hanger. Not one person in our class. The class was chanting, "Boney, Boney, Boney," as we walked up to the front hand in hand. Gail had sweaty hands, but I didn't mind. People didn't gross me out. I felt hot and wild, standing in front of the class, next to Mr. Groover. I was pleased to be seen right next to him, how did we look? It would be so much fun to be Mr. Groover's wife, grade his students' papers.

"Think Lemon Squeezer, hon," Mr. Groover said, and he patted my head, and he and Gail slipped the wire down. It went right down as I guided it. It was fun. I was standing in front of the class. I was looking at John who had this big stupid horse face, whiskers, and his fly open. I felt like Mr. Groover was making my clothes disappear.

My face was hot and red. Mr. Groover was smiling confidently, leaning on his desk as though this was what he had been waiting for all along. "Now you do it yourself, feet first, like you are entering the Glory Hole in Mammoth Cave, Kentucky, Georgia Jackson." I hopped into the wire circle and slipped it up, worming by body through it.

Andrew Hussman stood up and cupped his hands, "She's a stick! It's stick chick! She's not human!"

"Georgia, you are really gyrating," Carol Dean Moldenhauer warned me from her position in the front row.

Then Gail Cowert did it too, only she did it foot first and her dress slid up above her panties, for more than a few seconds, and she got tears in her eyes, but she wouldn't cry or run out, and I wanted to hug her. No one clapped; they were snickering. With her flip-flops slapping the cement floor, I gently led her back to her desk.

"You did it! You were great," I said. "You are way skinnier than me," I whispered to her, and I stroked the back of her hair, organizing it into calm tails, getting it to be straight so none of the hairs were crossing over their cousin hairs. She was mousy, my mother said. Don't play with her, it will only lead to problems. Didn't she have lice? Well, she did, but Mr. Groover had told us everyone got lice at some point, and we weren't going to be talking about it in this classroom at all.

Mr. Groover wrote our names on the boards under the words,

SPELUNKER CHAMPIONS OF 1979: GEORGIA JACKSON AND GAIL COWERT.

Gail and I walked home together that day.

We walked toward her house, the opposite way of my house, and held hands, and I told her I liked to imagine that when I spoke, what I said was in quotes. She didn't get that, and she didn't want to play like we were talking in quotes.

"Did you see the hanger hanging there on the window thingamajig?" she said. She was pulling on the side of her diamond print dress—all green and blue and gold diamonds stamped on the cheap cotton, balling the fabric up and wrinkling it and wetting it with her sweaty hand. It made the dress go way up her thighs, and I could see where she had burned herself.

"Yeah, I saw it," I said. I was walking her to her house, kind of dragging her—she was a slow walker. I wanted to go in badly and see it, where she slept and what they had in their fridge. But then I knew I'd be too scared; I had a feeling her father would be home.

"It looked like a big mouth," she said, "that hanger did."

I breathed out and let my shoulder touch hers, banging against her softly as we walked along, swinging our arms hard.

I looked at Gail's pale mouth, her teeth all crazy and sometimes brown like broken tiles, her bumpy skin, and I said, yeah it did, exactly like a mouth you could go in.

"And right back out," she said, and she spit on a bush. A real good honker. Good arc, good viscosity, is what Sid would have said.

"Eh, hey, kid," a tall, shirtless man said. He was sitting in his yard on a tree stump, next door to Gail's house.

"I hate that man," she said. "Next-door neighbors, ya know?"

"Yes," I said. "They're awful." I wished I had some examples. I was not used to friendship, and my mind went blank. But Gail didn't mind. She stood there, in her driveway, chewing on her hair, completely disorganizing it, grinning at me sweetly. She reminded me of a good cat, and there aren't too many of those.

I said, "See you tomorrow, friend." When I turned back to make sure she had gone in her house, I saw she hadn't. She was in that shirtless man's yard, and she was standing by him. Her head was back, and her mouth was open, and she must have been laughing.

I crossed Orange Avenue and headed home to tell my family about the new career I would pursue, cave explorer.

I got closer to home, and the breeze came off the lake and calmed me down. It was maybe the biggest school day of the year. I felt the wire had lit a little fire in me.

I felt so normal. I had a friend who needed me to save her from stump-sitting men, a future husband, a success, and a future. I scooted along, trying to walk all crisp and floaty like Jere Groover.

When I walked up the driveway, I noticed my father's car, his big brown-red Olds. Strange. Middle of the day, on a school day. It was strange. Like someone had died. I couldn't remember the last time I had seen him, exactly when that had been, and suddenly that made me start crying. What was I, crazy? Forgetting my father? Why was I so surprised to see him? Why hadn't I been *waiting* for him? I was so used to him being gone, I had forgotten to expect him. I longed for him, but it was autopilot longing, something I didn't have to think about. But I felt so guilty, the surprise of him, I'd burst into loud hot tears.

The Olds was running, but the lid to the trunk was up so the effect was of something snoring, something asleep, something that couldn't see but it was going on with its life as if it could. As if it could.

The door was locked, the front door, so I was banging on the bell when Sid came up behind me and grabbed my neck and said, "Welcome to the cracker factory. Will you be staying permanently?" He smelled like sugar and rubber and metal, and here I was, on my tiny body victory day, instantly wishing I was an Amazon pushing him to the ground and pinning him there with my big toe. I bit at his hands and started yelling for Mom.

"They're both in there," he said, pushing me off. "Chill, Georgie. Listen." He handed me a pack of Spree.

"What's Dad doing here?" I peeled the foil off the candy and popped the first one into my mouth. Lemon was not my favorite. "What's going on?" I said.

"What's he doing here? He's getting his stuff. He's moving out."

I realized I had thought he'd already moved out.

"Let's stop him," I said. "Sid, let's make a plan." We leaned against the front doors, big carved mahogany double doors, to our house.

"I hate it when you sound like fucking Pollyanna, that's who you think you sound like." Sid had this new way of flipping his hair out of his face, and he kept doing that, swishing his head around like a cool dude with a neck ailment.

The doors flung open, and my father stepped on us as we fell back onto the terrazzo floor, kind of laughing and scared.

"What are you kids doing, goddamn eavesdropping? What is this, what are you sneaking around like this for?" He was yelling.

"Whoa," Sid said. "Take it easy, old man."

"Daddy!" I said, trying to turn it back into the old days. I grabbed his leg. He shook me off, like I was dog.

He didn't look at me; he didn't even recognize me. His chest was sweating, and his face was red as a beet; you could see the blood inside of him was actually hot. His mustache was wet, his nose was running—his black eyes were striking us. "You kids. You aren't doing your homework. You should be in there getting it done before dinner, goddamnit. You're both not going to have any kind of future at this rate. I don't know what you're thinking," he said, and he stepped back from us. Sid went inside, walked away, and left me there to face him. He was in the courtyard now, and I was in the foyer, up the step, almost as tall as he was. I felt my head filling up with water.

"DON'T WALK AWAY FROM ME," he yelled into my face, at Sid, into the house behind me.

"It's not me," I said. "I'm not the one."

"Why did you even come back? We thought we were rid of you," Sid said. I wanted to hit him in the mouth.

"Please, for the sake of God, the neighbors," I heard my mother shriek from far inside the house.

"You're all nuts," my father said, and he threw his T-shirt onto the crown of thorns and tore off into the garage with his fists swinging. His car was still running, and I thought, this situation will run out of gas.

"What are you doing, Daddy?" I yelled, as I heard him flinging things around in the garage. I saw him walk out to his car with a box of tools and pants on hangers. He threw everything in the trunk, slammed it shut, lit a cigarette by leaning in his driver's side window and reaching down, and then he walked around the back of the house. "I'm not nuts," I shouted. I screamed it. I could hear my voice echoing, bouncing off the driveway, the other houses. "I'm not nuts!"

I figured Sid was comforting my poor mother, and so I went and lay down on the driveway. I tucked my tiny spelunking body behind the wheel of his car. I was almost long enough to be under both wheels. I didn't like the idea of my purple overalls on the black pavement, but I did like the idea of human sacrifice, of the way men and women in the Bible lie down on the ground at important junctures. I did like the idea of my father stopping on a dime, grabbing me in his arms, running back into the house, me limp, lifeless, my mother crying different tears, Sid wishing he had made a plan with me. I wished someone could see me— my long blonde hair on the pavement, me like an angel, the person who could fit through the tiniest spaces. This is what my most famous day had come to—me getting run over by my father. I scooched way up to the tire. There I was. The invisible woman, or the woman who gets cut in half, or Snow White—I was something. Some woman.

I'm so tiny, I thought, looking under the car at the pipes and ligaments, the rust, the pans that seemed to be too low to the ground, the feathers and bugs glued everywhere. Will I even be noticed? Will my body even cause a bump in my father's exit?

What happened happened fast. First, the front door slammed, and I didn't hear anything, no one seemed to come out, then the car door opened, slammed, the car radio blasted. I sat up, slid back, saw Sid's stupid head in the driver's seat and started yelping at him. The car rolled back, I got an amazing pinch, my chest, my shins, it was so amazing.

"Help, help," I screamed, but I couldn't even hear me. I rolled back. Miraculously, Sid put the car in forward as my father arrived at the side, and reached in the window and punched Sid and reached in with his other hand to turn off the car. Sid flew out the passenger's side and yelled that he wanted my father to leave, *we all did, hurry up and go, you're an alcoholic nightmare and we hate you.*

I got myself up; no one even knew I had nearly died for my country or my family or anything. I was standing there in the yard, yelling at my father, "We love you, don't leave, please don't leave, you aren't leaving for good are you?"

Mr. Underwood's head appeared at the wall, and he called over to us, "What is this, World War Three?"—making me realize my mother probably wouldn't want to live here anymore.

Then I dreamed so much. My sneaking through that wire. My holding hands with Gail Cowert, my vagina thinking so much about having Mr. Groover's babies come out of it; I was all wet between my legs by the time he got to talking about Karst topography and the formation of sinkholes. That was not important. I didn't care about that. He asked me to marry him. We lived on a houseboat. We never had to go in caves; we focused on the baking.

Late that night, my mom got me up for a horrible dinner.

My mother sobbed through the whole thing. Which made me mad because it was my day that deserved the stage.

"Georgia, no one cares," Sid said.

"But I am the skinniest person in my class. I won the contest today. I would like to have a friend over, can we?"

I felt that same heat coming out of me. The heat that came out when I was with Groover.

"Honey," my mother said. She looked at me like I was asking if I could sell myself into white slavery.

"Oh," I said. "I can't take this weird shit!"

"WHAT?" my mother screamed.

"*Stuff*, I said, *stuff. Stuff, stuff, stuff.*"

"That's not what I heard," my mother said. She still had her head on the table, her hair like an exploded salad over her plate.

"Please. Don't. Pressure. Me." My mother's mouth was a straight line. She pulled at her hair. "What's the point of eating anymore, what is the point, what is the point. What is the point, what is the point, what is the point."

She scraped her kitchen chair back from the table and ran down the hallway to her bedroom like a child. She locked the door and wouldn't come out, not even for Sid, not even when we begged her and left a bowl of hot tomato soup at the door.

It took me till Thanksgiving. Then, I got up my nerve. I complimented a girl I liked, Debbie James, who was perfect like Barbie, all smooth delicious swoops, her legs, her hips, her breasts, her lips. We were sitting in Mr. Groover's. He was lecturing on perpetual motion. During a lull, I said, "Debbie, I like your sundress. It's real pretty on you."

Debbie James looked at me like I was on the wrong side of the school—like I should have been on the retarded side all along, with the Sunshine children. Her chin dropped to her gorgeous neck, and her eyebrows lifted up into her bangs. Wings, the girls called bangs. *Are you retarded?* she said without speaking. *You are!*

To tell the truth, I had to agree with her.

Debbie and I got to sit next to each other because of the alphabet: Jackson, James. I was quite thrilled. Even though she hated me. I still liked her. She was so perfect, her nose like a sporty car, all swoopy and cute, her watery blue eyes, her long white hair, which she set on her breasts, in two even ropes. If I were a guy, I would have asked her out. She was rich, too.

Debbie had stared at me for a long time after I told her I liked her sundress. It was white with little pink flowers embroidered across her breasts and down one side, as though they were overwhelmed and had to get off that dress. Then, with her orchid blue eyes, she said, "Georgie, you're a lesbian?"

"Oh," I said. "Oh." My breath caught inside my throat and burned like rubber there. I didn't know what to say. I had an idea what she meant, but I didn't know how to begin, or how to end.

"Miss Jackson," Mr. Groover said. "I asked you to come up and label the armature."

"Is there a problem," Oscar Love said in a high mocking voice. He was looking at me grinning. I think he was thrilled I was getting in trouble. His long black hair fell in pieces, his leather jacket hung over his shoulders like a kite. Carol Dean was completely in love with him, but he was not her type. He was too cool for her. He traveled summers with his mom, in a flower-painted bus, selling leather crafts. The Loves were thrilling and wild and smart. It was funny that he was mocking me. I didn't think he even noticed.

"Can I?" Debbie said. "I can do it."

I ran, then, out of the classroom, because mucus was coming out of my nose, because I was crying.

Next day, I pretended it didn't happen. I drew swords in my science book. We had moved on to Energy: The Pulse of Life. We were doing fluorescence. During the quiz, Carol Dean Moldenhauer, queen of the geeks, asked Debbie to lunch. Debbie said, yes, Moldy, I would love to. Carol Dean lived on my street, three doors down. Her father was a minister. My mother hated men of the cloth because they were all hypocrites. I personally couldn't see anything wrong with the Moldenhauers, but I couldn't see what Debbie saw in Carol Dean. I guess she was Debbie's groupie, that was the bond.

I didn't have a single friend.

Gail had stopped coming to school. She was living, they said, with a man who had done electrical work at Walt Disney. Sometimes she got to go there free.

Lunch was the worst. I sat by myself. I ate my pudding and prayed no one would talk to me. I imagined various scenarios that could contain my father. Sid worked the parking lot, steering his dolly of candy around, selling, pocketing coins until his pouch was truly bulging. "George," he'd say. "How's it going, man? Doing all right?"

I was happy to have a cool brother. He had minions who followed him, keeping track of the sales, taking orders for cinnamon toothpicks, renting out Sid's python, which lived in our house and the science room, both.

"Don't look so sad, man." Sid looked pale and smart. He wore white dress shirts and cords. Not T-shirts, like every other kid. Like a serviceman. Which he was.

•

During lunch, the boys ate standing up, out in the parking lot. They smeared their pudding pops on the teachers' cars; they called each other pecker-puffer and peter-pumper pretty much the whole time. It was like overhearing wild birds, messing and calling, messing and calling. Repeating everything, like they were trying to figure out the secret of the universe by finding the right combination of words. Oscar never joined in; he played chess with a cool retarded kid named Rocko.

I missed Gail. I missed her questions. What is the difference between suck and blow? What do you think *smegma* really is?

The golden girls, Debbie and Lis Hagood and Amy Hobby and the others, stood in the sun, doing their hair. Boys came up to their knot, and there was a flush of laughter, and then the boys retreated, and a new pack was sent to the knot of girls, more laughter.

When Oscar Love sauntered up to the group on Friday, and they absorbed him in, I thought, well. Well, well, well. I got off the wall, and smoothing my red plaid skirt, I walked across the old basketball court, past the Sunshine kids, who were playing a wild game of freeze tag, but no one would stay frozen.

"Hey," I said, as I got close to the group of girls. Oscar was explaining something, pointing to the skies, and pointing to the asphalt. His denim shirt was unbuttoned except for one button at his navel. His jeans, bell-bottoms, were pale and thatchy with white threads, in contrast to the dark straight stovepipe Levis favored by every single one of my classmates, without exception.

"Hey," I said, louder. I slipped into the circle, right beside Carol Dean, who was laughing, her quiet rectangle mouth a large magenta gasp. *Ah ha ha ha,* silent air poured from her. I looked at her, looked at Oscar, flipped my hair over my shoulder, and was about to speak, no idea what, when Carol Dean grabbed my shoulder and pulled me back, out of the circle.

"Hey," I said, and I smiled at her. She was nice.

She motioned to the lunchroom. "Maybe go inside. You'll scare him away. Really."

"What? But I *know* Oscar."

"Yeah," she said. "But I want to know him better."

I stood there, the pavement burning through my shoes. I locked my eyes on hers, so she couldn't go back to her precious circle. But she did.

Because my mother answered the phone and said, "I don't think Georgia knows Carol Dean well enough—we don't want to intrude. I can ask her, but I'm afraid she will decline," I hollered out, "I want to, I'm doing it."

And that's how I found myself in Carol Dean's aboveground pool.

"Guess who is waiting for me," she said, thumping the vinyl side.

"Huh?" I said. I was making water angels, wanting Carol Dean to say something like, "You are really talented in the water."

She splashed water over the edge and told me to just stay cool if her mother came out. I could see her mother through their plate-glass window, in front of the television, doing cross-stitch in her lap. Mrs. Moldenhauer was kind and beautiful.

Carol flung herself over the edge of the pool and burst into high cooing laughter. "I can't believe you," she said.

I still thought she was talking to me. The way I swam, the way I had plunked all my hair on my head in a large cone.

"Oscar," she said, and at this moment I leaned way over the edge of the pool, and under the shade of the oaks, there was Carol, her top already off, and Oscar under her, his floral bell-bottoms and his mesh tank top soaked in places, dry in others.

"I—" I said, but they didn't look up. Should I pretend I hadn't seen this. I whipped around. Mrs. Moldenhauer hadn't moved a muscle. She was like a statue, like the white pleated lampshade, or the cement angel.

Carol Dean rubbed her hands up and down Oscar's body, even across the front of him, between his legs. His face was up in hers, they were kissing, and his sideburns, his hair, his hands—he looked all rough and unusual for a ninth grader. How long had this been going on?

My heart felt like it had an incision.

"It's the only way we get to see each other. You're a *great* distraction." Carol wasn't looking at me, she was lying on top of Oscar, whose back ground into the mucky grass there. But she talked like we were in typing class.

I shoved a wave of water on them. They both laughed. I didn't understand what to do. I had exhausted my repertoire.

"Y'all are sick," I said. They were wrapped around each other. He had one hand on her breasts, pushing them together and one hand down between her legs. She was on the bottom now. Her hair was going to be muddy. I lay on the bottom of the pool for a moment, and then I whooshed up, and yelled for Mrs. Moldenhauer. "Mrs. Moldy! We need you! Mrs. Moldy! We need you out here a sec!" Then I lay back down on the bottom of the pool, watching the water above me swirl and swish. I was a dish at the bottom of the sink. A simple dish, waiting its turn to be washed. Carol leaped back into the pool, submerged to her neck, and asked me to help her tie her top. I straightened her green bottoms, too, which were all wonky on her. A whirl of black water, from her mud, coursed out around us. Mrs. Moldenhauer gave us white towels she'd warmed in the dryer. They were the largest towels I had ever seen. She packed us off to the shower, and Carol Dean and I showered together. I tried not to look at her breasts, but I couldn't help but stare at them. I had never showered with a person. It was so strange. Carol acted like she did this all the time. I helped her rinse the Oscar-mud out of her hair.

We had real tea, with cream and brown sugar, poured from a green flowered teapot. Carol's mother sat with us at the table, and I talked, nonstop. When Mrs. Moldy asked if we would like to work on the practice pre-SAT book together, I said sure, yes, of course, I'd been hoping she would ask, even though I had no idea what she was talking about.

Carol Dean loaned me a green blouse and a pair of jeans. I saw her look out the back window for Oscar whenever Mrs. Moldenhauer was getting us pencils, or crackers, or magazines so we wouldn't mar the table.

"Are you going to marry him?" I whispered to her.

"I don't know," she said, and she showed me a bracelet she kept in her pocket, always, an ID bracelet he'd given her. "They aren't Christians, you know."

"I know," I said. "That's the only thing my mom likes about him and that family."

Carol Dean didn't laugh like I thought she would, so I did. "Just kidding," I said. I slapped her arm.

Mrs. Moldenhauer sat with us and shelled peas for their dinner. She invited me to stay. I said I couldn't, but maybe another time.

"Just call your mom!" Carol Dean said, handing me the phone.

"I can't," I said. "I have to help her tonight."

"Help her what?" Carol Dean said, popping raw peas into her mouth.

"You have really struggled, haven't you, Georgia," Mrs. Moldenhauer said. "Is the divorce final?"

"What?" I looked out the window, where a cardinal was fluffing itself on their feeder.

A buzzer went off in the carport, and Mrs. Moldenhauer told Carol Dean to go pull the laundry out of the dryer.

I didn't want to think. I wanted to go home. My mother would die if she knew people thought they were getting a divorce. She threw anything from Buck's lawyers straight into the trash.

I opened the pre-SAT book, and there was a list of colleges with their college codes. Florida State University, 987379. University of Central Florida, 098363. I'd had no idea there were so many colleges in the world. I wanted to memorize those codes.

I looked into Mrs. Moldenhauer's soft eyes, but I didn't hear a word of what she was saying to me. I was seeing Oscar.

I wanted Oscar to kiss me and kiss me and kiss me until I sunk. I couldn't love Mr. Groover anymore. Carol Dean had literally rubbed off on me. In the shower. In the pool. I wanted what she had. I was happy about it. I wanted Oscar. I wanted him to marry me. Carol Dean would be done with him, I figured, in a short time. I would bide my time.

"Did you hear me?"

"Yes," I lied. "It all sounds good." I imagined Oscar's tongue down my throat while I took a sip of Moldy's tea. On that day, and for a lot of days after, Oscar seemed to me like the only thing that would feel good.

"Girls, you two should take sewing together. Be buddies."

"Yes!" said Carol Dean. She actually clapped her hands together. She acted like she was in a book.

"I'll walk you home, then," Carol announced.

For the first time in my life, I knew exactly what to do.

Gulf of Mexico

Buck Jackson had a thousand dollars in his wallet. In hundreds. Ten hundred dollars.

He had divested himself of change.

It was Saturday. Hotter than hell and humid as an armpit. Florida. Dee-*lish*.

Buck went the exact speed limit, plus ten mph. Always. His mouth tasted like metal bananas. He turned up the AC, wished it went higher. Ashes fluttered. The highway seemed to fairly pull the Fairmont along. He flicked on the autopilot. Buck pressed back into the spongy vinyl seat and felt his kidneys compress. His thighs managed the wheel.

He thought: *all my skillets are sitting in the sink, rusting. The woman in my bed will wash up, she'll wash up, nose around, and be there when I come home with a cooler of fish.*

Buck Jackson collected different things—dolls, cans, pans, vintage signage . . . and he felt around on the seats, the dash, under his seat, for mouthwash. Empty gin bottles. He spit on his palm and looked at the stuff. He sniffed it. It was like epoxy, pungent and animal-glorious. He felt locked in by stuff, and that he couldn't get to Pine Island for the fishing with his brothers, couldn't get there soon enough.

Every mile of I-4 was spattered with black oil mirages; he drove to the edge of each icky pool, and it disappeared. Then he flew through seeming water. He'd be down at Pine Island by 4:00 P.M. A long tooth of an island in the gulf, Pine Island supported his brothers who were waiting, drinking, ensconced in the Pink Indian bar.

Geno's ranch, Misty Pines, flourished on the north end of the island. Brother Donald whiled away the days faking in his wheelchair, roaming the sandy streets of Bokelia, the old town, old shipping site of gator hides, oranges, and furs. Best fishing camp in the world; Buck'd caught more snook there than his brothers combined, and they lived there year-*round*.

He hit the horn, riding it to pass three chicken trucks. He caught the scent of perfume on his hand.

Dottie Dee—he could see her stretched out on his super-king adjustamatic bed—like a car wreck, the black satin in a tangle. He'd told her he was leaving for the weekend, but he doubted Dottie Dee heard. She was his main squeeze and had many cancers in her. She was using a cane. Dottie Dee, like most, had selective hearing. He couldn't see how'd she be a great accountant, but that's what she did. Books for a taxidermy outfit. Her skills, he was sure, remained elsewhere. Though they hadn't ever actually made love, she slept at his house. He slept on the couch.

"Holy shit," he said. "Fuck!"

He'd run up on a mother in a wagon. He flashed his lights, four times, and honked. He laid on the horn again. She was oblivious.

"Move it, hon! Move it or lose it!"

Mothers in wagons habitually clogged the passing lane. They didn't know. They pissed away the days, hauling the bitty-bits around, royal rulers, crumb-crunchers. He slammed on the horn, waved both hands, cursed his broken, stuck-in-the-up-position window. "Move it, lard ass!" he screamed.

He'd make Pine Island by 5:00 P.M.

Happy hour specials at the bar, where his brothers Donny and Geno were no doubt already socked in, the idiots. Geno was a wino, fancied himself a fancier. Donny drank to wash down pills. Both brothers were mental deficients.

Donny'd been a bed-wetter well through junior high.

Geno had dropped out, 'bout the same time, gone into all kinda schemes. Made a buttload of money, all of it dirty: emu, ostrich, sisal, hemp, apartment complexes, rearview mirrors, now the cattle ranch and fish ladders. On a big old ranch on a small island in the Gulf of Mexico. It was a song, wasn't it? *I been all around the world, to the Gulf of Mexico....*

Geno was the kind of man who didn't deserve to be rich. Geno looked like Kenny Rogers: panther-gray hat, thick bush of a beard, a big slab of a man—sparkling eyes set into crinkled nests, eyebrows like moss. Geno'd got the looks. Buck had the brains. Donny had the audacity, the bad luck, a heap of boy kids, and more addictions than states in the union.

Again, Buck laid on his horn. "Fucking road hog!" Buck rolled down the passenger window, veering wildly into the truck's lane. "Who the hell do you think ya are, God?"

He flicked off his sunglasses and talked to the Fairmont in front of him. Like his car, only blue. His was yellow. He checked the hood. Yup.

Yellow. Why in the world he had bought a yellow car, he didn't know. He didn't remember buying it.

Then a Landau cut him off.

Buck slammed on his horn and his brakes. "Some of us have lives!"

He felt like coming to a standstill, on I-4—this was sheer lunacy. "What the fuck is this shit?" Instead he gunned it.

He banged on his steering wheel, flicked off the cute pussy in the Landau. She drove exactly like his ex-wife, Mary Carol. "Get off the road!" he yelled. He needed to fix his driver's side window. It was unsafe, driving with that window stuck in the up position, and the crack driving him crazy, the wind buzzing his hair; but worse was the noise, the constant whine. The lack of ability to roll it down and scream out of it.

Buck had known himself to be always a sensitive person. He had fine nerves. He could feel them. They all met up in his stomach, in a grand convention of energy. He was a fragile man. "A lover, not a fighter," he said.

Then for a while he held ninety-five, steering with his knees, passing the asshole truckers. Donny'd been a trucker before he jackknifed, killing his wife and oldest son. Donny used a chair now, but more for kicks than anything. He'd gotten addicted to pills during his recovery. The man didn't know hard work. Parents had spoiled him. Then he never seemed to accept the loss of Nora and Caleb. He never got over it. A broken man, that was Donald. Not a pretty sight.

Buck was considering the Geno situation—the horses, the cow trading, the pork bellies, Geno's money—figuring the man was behind on his taxes and that was why his development on the north end of the island had slowed to standstill. Buck was considering how he could buy in, kiss Geno's ass, or fuck it, or both, or kick back and have some fun with the brothers, when the gumball machine lit up his rearview.

"Oh, for God's sake," he said. "Pinched." Then he thought he needed to get out of the way so the pig could arrest the asshole in front of him. But when he pulled onto the shoulder, not slowing, chunking along, forcing the Fairmont to vibrate in a creepy alluring way, the officer followed and then started up his goddamn siren.

"Si-*rene*," Buck said, mystified, looking back and slowing. "Sirene?" He liked to say it so it rhymed with "Irene." He wiped his brow. "Whelp, it will be most interesting to see what the fuck this yay-hoo is after." He had a rifle and a couple cases of Old Milwaukee in the trunk.

The cop stared through the permanently-up driver's side window. Buck looked up at him, cocked.

"Fine day, isn't it." Buck grinned.

The officer was twelve years old, with a blond Nazi haircut, those tough-ass aviator glasses.

"Probably cost the county two hundred bucks, am I right?" Buck spoke calmly through his rolled-up window.

"Please, slowly lower your window, sir, and I need license, registration, proof of—"

Buck didn't know what the asshole was saying because he couldn't hear, and the Nazi dick didn't move his lips when he talked. Buck assumed the boy was saying something to this effect.

"Goddamn, my window's broken. Obviously."

"Excuse me?" The cop stepped back one large step and tucked his chin, talked into his radio, all serious and impassive-like.

Officer Broom—you'd think he'd change his name for the tag— rapped on the glass and then started signaling Buck—some mysterious rounded motion, and Broom was back on his radio. Buck could see himself, in his yellow Fairmont, a fisherman, a man who looked like he was underwater, bent through the glass. A man within a man within a submarine.

"For God's sake. You want me to do a cartwheel." Buck heard a helicopter and felt himself gag. He started across the seat, sliding over the old beer can, the map folio, the sunglasses from other girlfriends or his daughter—what a mess. But then he thought, I can get out of my own fucking car.

When he put his hand on the handle, Broom shouted, "PUT YOUR HANDS OVER YOUR HEAD."

"Oh, so we do have a voice," Buck said. "Couldn't hear you *whispering* before."

Pressing the door open, feeling a hot pocket of Florida air rush in, like a disease, Buck swung his feet off the pedals. He felt his gastrointestinal juices gracefully moving up and down his tube.

Broom was in a SWAT stance, crouched, his gun pointed at Buck's head.

"I'm a peace-loving man," Buck said. The kid smelled like peaches and cream. He was like schnapps. He was nothing, he was a baby, a pussy. Buck planted his feet on the gravelly shoulder and took in some of the hot air.

"Mr. Jackson, I'm going to need you to step out of the car."

"Oh, come on, kid. Ya gotta be kidding me." Buck lurched out of the car, blinking in the hot steady sun. Traffic sped past.

The cop made him recite his name and address. He took the paperwork and Buck's license back to his bright blue flashing vehicle.

Buck grinned back at him and stood at the side of the highway with his hands over his head. He stuck his thumb out.

Then he walked over to the ditch, went to unzip his fly, found it unzipped, and he took a piss. When he returned, Broom made him do a Breathalyzer.

"Oh, God. I have to go through that ordeal? What happens if I refuse? I can refuse." A rash of honking ensued. "Thank you, my fellow citizenry!" Buck hollered. Broom fiddled with buttons on the breath gizmo. It was a computer with a white plastic straw sticking out.

Buck threw his arms back up to the heavens. "I happen to be partial to the First Amendment of our fine constitution, which I'd wager you've never even read, kid." Buck hocked spit into the highway.

Broom bopped over to the grass. "That's a civil infraction, and it is your right and it's two hundred dollars. If you refuse the breath test." Broom acted as though he'd had to say this so many times, it was a chore to repeat it.

"Where do I blow, asshole?" Buck swaggered over to the grass, leaned over Broom's palms, and sucked in a little air. Buck saw an alligator down in the ditch, behind his car. He smiled, and then he laughed.

"Harder," Broom said. "*Blow* harder. Don't let it leak out. Don't suck."

It was a fat short straw, like for a baby. Fat, hard, and stout. Broom read the numbers.

"Keep doing it."

"What do you think I am? A camel?"

"No sir, no. But now we have to start over." He yanked the straw back, fiddled with the numbers, and stuck it back in Buck's mouth. "Don't talk. A camel?"

Buck felt the sun on his bald spot—he had that sensation of being a griddle. He felt oily and denuded, as though the sun were cooking some part of him, something exposed.

"When was your last drink?"

Buck looked at him from under his giant caterpillar eyebrows, blowing all the while.

Finally, he was done.

"I think this machine is acting up. It says you're fine. It says you are in great shape."

"What's your ID number? I'm reporting your assholery, your harassment, your illegal accostment... this is a charade. It's a tirade. I know the state's attorney general as a personal friend; he'll hear about this, Broom, ass-wipe. This is an egregious—"

"You want this to be assault?"

"I'm a peace-loving man, bro. I'm Colonel Buck Jackson, a peace-loving man."

Buck tore up the ticket and let the wind fondle it out the working window, into the ditch. Snack for the gator, little pink slip for the big boys. "For crying out loud," he said.

Then Buck sped down the highway, crossed the Polk County line, and whooped. He was thirsty.

It was definitely *time* for a drink.

Donny Osmond was on the radio, and Buck was, oddly, mildly in the mood for faggy.

He popped a warm one. Oh, life is good, he said. Then Paul Harvey came on. Not this, he said aloud. I could do better than this. He found Kenny Rogers. Then he found a gospel station. Black gospel. The real thing. He sang along, his voice beautiful to himself, working his way into knowing the words as each one came over the radio scratch to him.

He could close his eyes, let the car fling itself down the highway, over the rickety bridge, through the Indian town, past the fish camp, down the two-track, around the slope of the island, out to the gulf sea. It was a beautiful place. Greeks, Indians, real authentic types lived here. Men who lived off the sea, the elements. Men who fished. Buck fished. He was thinking of his sailfish now. He'd been in the paper that year. His taxidermist let the fish rot, but he had the article somewheres. JACKSON'S SAIL, read the subhead. It was a glorious picture except he looked like he weighed more than the fish, which had not been the case at all.

When he walked into the Captain—the shack beach bar at the south end of Pine Island—that evening, he was in that perfect narrow band. It was a perfect buzz. Like the radio when you are high enough above sea level and your sunglasses are real clean, and so is your windshield. You are clear and soft—every hundred or so drunks, he gets that. Perfection. It's what keeps him drinking. Why everyone should drink.

The Captain is dark—even darker than it is outside—the stars on the island are bright, hot-looking in the mottled evening sky. Buck doesn't wait for his eyes to adjust. Sunglasses on, he walks straight in. Bumping into people is a good way to acclimate—better than shyly looking around and getting all freaky-deaky. Sizing up this, sizing up that. Buck likes the rush you get from walking into a dark room, across a dark dance floor.

Voilà.

"Where are the boys?" Buck calls out. He is sure Nib will remember him, but Nib doesn't even turn around. "My brothers? Tweedle Dee and Tweedle Stupid?" First thing Donny would say to him would be, "Did you lay some pipe last night?"

A woman in a black bathing suit, sagging boobs, and a burned face tells him Donald left hours ago. "Like I'm thinking lunch? For the Indian? Something? Cuz that boat guy come in here and wanted his three thousand dollars from Donaldo, and that—"

"Thank you?" Buck says, mocking her, curtsying, taking his glass of gin off the bar, out to his car. After draining the weak drink, he sets it nicely on the cement retaining wall alongside the bar. The sea slapping, slapping, makes him feel dizzy, makes him feel he's falling, or falling in.

Buck feels strong entering the Pink Indian. As the woman at the Captain's bar predicted, there is his brother. Buck sidles up to Donny pretending to be like a seductive woman. Buck runs his hands through Donald's nappy hair. He can feel his fat brother-man breathing in the dank beery light. The Clydesdales are chugging about the barrel, and Donny is right below them, as though wearing a hat of horses.

"Hey," Donny says in a furry voice.

Buck hits him flat across the butt. Which of course has no impact since Donny weighs three hundred.

"Have you fucking *gained*, brother? You look to weigh two-fifty, man."

Donny ignores him. He is talking to the television. Donny's well connected with life on other planets. *Charlie's Angels* is a good way to stay in touch. "Hey, bro," Donny says when the commercial comes on.

"So," Buck says, signaling the bartender, getting no response, "my trip started out disastrously, being that I forget the poles, and then it got worse from there."

Buck talks on. He has tried to analyze the criteria of the perfect buzz with many friends. Some people think it is food. Some people think it is sex. Some people think it is God. Buck thinks it is the exact right amount of sleep, not too much. Not too little. But better too little than too much. He likes to be up early. He likes to beat dawn.

"Where's Geno?" Donny finally says when the commercial goes off.

"I thought he was with you—"

"He's not."

"You haven't heard a word I've said," Buck says.

"Neither have you. Buy us some pigs' feet to gnaw on, bro. Buy us some nachos. They got nachos here."

"They don't have nachos here. Are you nuts?"

"They have nuts, too. Let's get nuts and nachos. I'm starved."

"You don't need to eat. You don't need to eat for a coupla months." Buck's getting anxious for the bartender to set him up. The bartender's in the back. "Martin," Buck yells. He hates to be an asshole, but after a point, come on.

Donald reaches over with fat damp hands, the color of conchs, and smoothes Buck's wild eyebrows. "You look like a psychokiller," Donny says.

"What do you say shit like that for." Buck strains to see the eyebrows in the bar mirror.

Donny orders Boodles.

"Don't have it." Martin slaps his hands on the counter as though he is impatient. Buck looks around. Even in the shadows, he can see—two guys at the pool table, a bimbo leaning on the jukebox, looking lonely and dancey, and him, and Donald. Buck wonders why he acts busy when he's clearly hanging on by a thread?

"Stoli? You don't *have* Stoli? Captain. *Oh my Captain!* You are a disgrace to the bartending race!" Donny shouts.

"I'm having a Bud. I'm a simple man," Buck says. He is surprised the bartender does not want to hear his Cajun joke. A good joke you want to hear over and over. It's a good joke.

"Donny," Buck says, kicking the chair-cum-footstool out from under his feet, which causes it to fold up, like a cheesy accordion, "Why you drinking premium? You have no job! What be wrong with your head?"

"Oils the chair," Donny says. "Better than that pisswater." He goes to explain Geno's new shipment of Chilean merlot vastly exceeds the previous shipment of Australian crap in body and nose. "It's cheaper in the long run to drink the good stuff, you know; that's basic macro-economic strategizing, big bro."

"Did you lay any pipe last night?" Donald asks him, nicely.

"Oh, come on, now." Buck breathes out slowly. "This is art in fermented form." Buck takes a long slip of beer into his mouth. He's never gone in for the whole wine-snob deal. Lotta money, not a lotta bang for the buck. Merlot, Cabernet, Riesling. He knows his way around a wine cellar, but who cares. He'd rather be fishing. Wine's a bit showy for his taste. "Where's Geno you say? We getting a night charter? Is old Emilio around? He taking us out? I came here to fish!"

"I said our good Brother Eugene was taken, in a beam of white light, to a planet where all the women suck dick, that's all they do. Is what I said, bro."

"Oh," Buck says.

They finish their drinks, get more.

Buck can't get settled down, though. He wants to go out into the ocean, he wants to be sitting on the sea, with his drink, with a coupla fishing poles going. He wants to be *doing*. "Drive to the ranch?" He says it again to Don, but Don is head down on the bar, napping now.

Buck observes the dancey woman in a halter top she really shouldn't be wearing. Her blonde hair is like waffles—puffed out in wayward pillows, a tiny checkery of them, and sprayed hard. That could be the syrup. He wants to touch her. He wants to feel her skin. It will be skin that has spent too much time in the sun. Her eyes are dark blonde, her hair pad waffle blonde. She's all pooching out in the boob and the butt—a hot little handful. Buck laughs. Women are so stupid.

The woman is dancing with the jukebox. Why do women do this? Why do they feel the urge to wiggle? It amuses Buck. Everyone in the world is so willing to make a fool of him- or herself.

"Born to be fucked," he says to Donny, raising his eyes up. He kicks Donny.

"Yeah, we should get on up to the other end of the island." Donny is up, pert, like he was never MIA. "But I think Geno said he was meeting us here, Boss. I think he did. I know he did." Donny, who is sitting now backward on two stools, with his wheelchair acting as a footrest, shouts to the bartender who is dusting the fan blades over the dance floor. Shafts of dust turn green and violet in the beer light. "Where's my brother? I am his keeper! Martin. Get me Gene Jackson, get me that rich ass uh-gully Jackson boy. Get him now."

"Keep it down, will ya?" Buck bangs Donny on the head.

"Fuck off, bro," Donny says. "You have this attitude, man. You come down here." Donny has finished the plastic plate of nachos in a vacuum.

"What the hell are you talking about?"

"You think you are this sort of, I don't know, this force—"

"What the hell?" Buck swings around, puts his feet down, and looks at his brother's cockeyed face. It's a white plank of flesh, cut up, rusty, stained. His eyes are liquid flesh. Donny's mustache is way too long, uneven, a handlebar on a broken bike.

"So what are you gonna do, hit me now, Buck?" Donny laughs hard, and says he's gonna pee.

"You don't work. You mooch, you drive Geno—"

Donny stands up, abruptly, which, even though Buck knows the wheelchair is an act, makes him reach out for Donny, to aid him.

Donny hunkers a roundhouse punch into the side of Buck's left jaw, and he takes two stools down with him.

The boopsie doodle comes rushing over, and when Donny leans down—Buck is totally conscious and now also sober. He can feel all the peanut shells on his backside, stuck on his seat, to the sweat on his neck.

Donny says, sneering, "You little no-shit piece of—" and Buck lunges up, grabs his neck, and tries to slam his head down onto the floor. Which is hard, because Donny is on his knees, like a large coffee table, and Buck is more like the rug.

"Hey y'all, hey y'all, hey y'all, come on, now, come on." She is screaming, her voice high and windy.

The hand on the back of his neck, a meaty cold hand, is also pulling Donny off him. It's not Martin, who is yelling at them to get the hell out of his place.

"I came to fish," Buck says. "I'm a peace-loving man!" The girl is handing him a wet towel, which he would no more wipe on his face than used toilet paper. "Hon," he says.

"Geno!" Donny says. All is forgotten. Drugs have rotted the man's head.

"Hey," Buck says.

Geno, looking more like Kenny Rogers than ever before, holds the two collars of the two brothers. He's muscular, tall, heavyset. He has three gold necklaces on his chest, sparkling in the gray hair there. He's wearing a rug.

"Nice rug," Buck says, pulling at it. Geno pushes him away, and Buck feels like a fish. Geno's sparkly blue eyes crinkle and wink. Geno looks prosperous. His belt buckle is coated with gold ropes.

"Let's go fish," Buck says. He is thirsty.

"Your brother fucking tried to kill me," Donny says.

"Donny, damn if you're not a hothouse flower. Get your fucking hands off me, Gene," Buck says. He takes charge of the situation. Geno steers them, in one fell swoop to the bar, sits them down. Martin sets them all three up.

"On me," Geno says. He moves to the women at the other end of the bar, where clearly he has been in conversation for some time.

"I didn't see him, did you?" Donny says. "Sittin' there, this whole time? Why would he not talk to us?"

"For God's sake, bro." He asks for an order of fried mullet, and Donny says to order him one too. "You got no money. Donny—"

"—And give us a coupla dozen oysters, raw, and some fried conch, too, wouldya Marty."

"I guess this is dinner. I guess we'll have to get up early to fish. We can go at 4:00 A.M. We should go hit the hay. You trying to get some livestock for tonight?"

Donny lolls his head back.

"Are you having a stroke?" Buck shrugs at the shuddering Donald.

Geno's two women, Mrs. Plaster and Mim Satterwhite, are well known to Buck. They had a vacation place on the jetty, the Satterwhites did. Bud Satterwhite was nowhere to be seen, and Buck thought Geno probably serviced the missus.

Meanwhile, Geno's wife, Angie, was likely down at Palm Beach, shopping her pert ass off. Shopping.

"Hello, friends," Buck said. He popped a couple of oysters in his mouth, lifted his glass to the trio in the shadows. "Anyone up for a dance?" Hank Williams had come on the juke. "Come on, Mim. Up!" He wiped his mouth, put in two conch fritters. "These are good, Mart."

Buck yanked Mim up. Mr. Plaster came in the door at this point, and both he and Mrs. Plaster smiled in that polite way that annoyed Buck—like they were shy and critical, both at once. "Loosen up! Friday night!" He pulled at the woman's arms until she rose up from the stool. "Geno. When I get back from cutting the rug, I want to talk to you about a little investment idea I think you will be quite interested in."

Geno smiled at Buck, winked. The man had the effect of being windblown, somehow, even when he was sitting still. Sexy as hell. *I have one sexy brother,* Buck thought. "Drive down okay, hoss?" Geno said.

"No, it was a disaster. I got pinched. I'll appeal that."

Mim's stool fell over, and her purse spilled. No one moved to straighten out that situation; Buck spun her around the floor of the Pink Indian. The floor was sticky parquet, shellacked like a boat, and Buck danced Astaire-like, trying help to Mim out. Sometimes she had the beat, sometimes she didn't. When new rock came on, Lynyrd Skynyrd, someone helpful yelled from the bar. The place was filling up now, smoke thick and the smell of stale beer from dirty taps like uncomfortable blankets. Buck said, "How do ya dance to this shit?"

"Yes, whatever it takes."

"Where's your dufus?"

"What?"

"Where's your dufus? Your worse half? Your significant otherly?"

"Who?"

"Where's your husband?"

"Sitting right over there."

"I'll go tell him to come in."

"Don't *bother*." She stopped dancing—they were still the only two on the floor. He noticed then she was wearing a bright red and white polka-dotted dress.

"You're not going to live to be a hundred, nothing you can do to stop bopping the clock, honey. Dance one more? You look good."

"I'm beat."

Buck clicked his heels and did a swooping soft-shoe, his hands like cartwheels, his feet like a combine. He was an amazing dancer. "You don't get the beat, honey." Out of the corner of his eye, he saw Donald, finishing off the tray of food. "I'm going to get Satterwhite in here. What's he doing all that pouting like some pussy?"

"What?" Mim went back to a stool, on the other side of her husband. Buck yelled at her that she'd done a good job, and thank you much for the dance. "Next!" he hollered to the bar at large.

The dancey waffle chick came up to him. He performed his super-low hoedown step. She knelt down in front of him, shimmied up into his arms, and Buck waved old Mim off, after giving her a steering shove toward her still-toppled stool. The Plasters were now engaged in conversation with the suits from the city who'd that minute walked in. Plaster was running for judge of Hendry County. Mr. Big. *What an asshole,* Buck thought. He'd himself make a fine judge; he had an innate sense of the law. Hell, he'd been a judge basically his whole life. That was Buck's problem. He was too nice. Too honest. Too much on the side of common sense and clean living. Too willing to intervene in a complex situation and straighten out the ailing party, the failing, weaker, dumber nuts.

"I'm a nut magnet," he said to Bouncey. He was winging her around the parquet. It was fun. They were going fast. They were wild. She sure could dance. She was leading now. He felt he was smooth, and he added some kicking. She was laughing and laughing. He saw in her eyes, brown eyes, rounder than a squirrel's, an unhinged look. Round the edges. He flung her into the tables, whoops. Then he recaptured her. He was the fun brother. The fat one, the mean one, the fun one.

"Jackson boys come to the island to party a bit," he said. "Do you fish?"

"What ya got?" she said. Her lips were chapped, like white shells.

Buck had gone outside to piss in the sea, and soon Donny was standing there, his wheelchair under one foot, cooing in the dark sparkly night.

"Hammish say eet's time to go, eet's time to go, boy!" Donny made his face a mouse face.

"Geno's coming? We got to get to bed if we're going to do any reasonable fishing tomorrow. We can't leave at noon, like last time. Last time was an unmitigated disaster, if you will remember—"

"Hammish say eet's time! Time go!"

"What's his problem. You know? What the hell's the holdup? This kind of thing. It doesn't make any sense to me." Buck shoved the wheelchair in the trunk of his car, and his trunk wouldn't close. Donny got in his car, oblivious, as though Buck were his servant. The wheelchair stuck out at angles like a grasshopper, not a good grasshopper.

Buck turned to Geno's car, glancing over his shoulder every other second or so, willing his brother, pompous boy, to come out and get a move on. Not that Buck wanted to be anywhere, merely wanted to be moving, before the night completely died, flatlined. He wondered if they even would be able to get Geno and Donny both up, fed, processed, and into a charter boat in the early hours.

Buck heard the waves slapping on the retaining wall. The Pink Indian was filled with people, but it seemed dead. No one was in the parking lot. He was alone. His trunk lid was flapping in the wind. Scraping the wheelchair, metal on metal.

"Bungee?" Buck said. "Cord?" He made bungee cord outlines with his hands in the night.

Half an hour later, Plaster, Satterwhite, and Geno sat packed in the new red Cadillac, whooshing down the thin road along the sea break. The two women were in the front seat with Kenny Rogers himself, and the two men sat in the back.

They looked quite the picture in the moonlight, the water like a dreamy moonscape itself in the backdrop, the sound of the waves slapping the breakfront.

Buck kept up with Geno, who was weaving like a lunatic—he had to be kidding, trying to get Buck's goat, which he was doing successfully.

Donald produced a bottle of Kahlua.

"Geez," Buck said. "Where'd you come up with that?" He took a long swig. Geno roared ahead. "Dangerous living, man. How do y'all make it home every night."

"We often don't."

"Don't drink it all," Buck said. The stuff smelled too sweet to him.

Geno was tearing up Caloosahatchee like a bat out of Hades.

"Jesus, bro," Buck said, loud. "Look at him!"

"He does this every night. The car is trained. It cost him two grand extra, but the vehicle is programmed to chart the shortest, safest course from Captain's or Injun to Angie's bed."

"We were at the Pink Indian. Does it know that?"

"We should stop in at Captain and see how he's doing, if he had a good night. You know, Captain got a fourteen-year-old girl pregnant, a summer girl? From Mackinaw Island, I think the girl was. You hear that?"

Donny coughed for a good mile. Buck sped up, to shepherd his brother. He wasn't sure he could remember the turnoff to the ranch.

Cars were coming from the other way—it was 3 A.M. The bars on the island had all let out.

The enveloping dark seemed to snatch the cars along, absorbing the Cadillac ahead, and the Landau, too, in its wake.

Buck fiddled with the radio. He drove well when he had a rhythm. He couldn't feel his body. With the music, which he couldn't locate on the shit radio, he would drive straighter. "Sing, asshole," he said to Donny. Donny snored in response. It smelled as though Donny peed his pants, too.

"Gawd," Buck said. He was the smartest brother. "I think this is where I want to buy that piece of property," Buck said. "I love this low-lying spot, right here, right past this corner. I think. Behind them pines. Isn't that the spot I was looking at a couple years back? I should've bought it then when I had the money."

Geno sped up, as though to keep Buck from getting a glimpse at his piece of paradise. They were now going sixty or so. Buck wiped the sweat off his own forehead and wiped each hand, slowly, down his pant leg.

"You want to fuck some hot pussy," Donny said. His eyes were closed. His skin looked like granite in the blackness. That was the last thing Donny said for a long, long time.

Geno's Cadillac's taillights slipped around the corner, where the waterfront road curled back down the main spine of the island. Geno had weird taillights—three red circles on each side. Six red dots, like the dots on old Boopsie's dress—the six dots—but what Buck was seeing was wrong dots.

He leaned forward, held his breath, concentrated every part of him on looking ahead through the gritty windshield.

The road had curved left, toward the sea, curling close along the water, and somehow, though Buck's eyes were half-open and he couldn't see, he really couldn't see anything much, he saw the dots and he knew. Geno's taillights had disappeared. Buck saw the headlights—

he could always tell Cadillac headlights, always—then turning, right, to the right, and then slipping over the left, over the break wall, the lights, like a slow sad meteor, a shooting star way too low and too short.

Sideways, all wrong, and then nothing, nothing at all.

Buck, sober, said, "No. No, no." He felt no relief. He felt he'd run over small children, a palette of them, and he could feel shouts in his organ, in his heart.

Buck drives 500 feet, 1000 feet, a mile, past the curve, left curve—on the right side of the road it's all thick palmetto scrub; there is nowhere to pull over. It's a godforsaken place. He never bought property here for that reason. He finds a driveway. He flings himself out of the car. Donald cannot be roused.

Buck wonders if he himself is alive.

The pavement is still warm. Heat comes off his car. Too much heat. He pats himself down—he hasn't got what he needs, and he can't shake that feeling.

Crisp and fast, Buck runs back up the road, to the rocks, which seem red to him. They aren't there; he can't see the car. It's twelve feet deep and rocky here. This side of the island gets the weather. There aren't rocks. Then it's a dock, a tethered boat, and then he can't run anymore and he can't see. He can hear the sea. He kneels in the road.

What the hell. Is Geno back now at his ranch, having a good brandy, the women passing salted nuts, Mim playing the piano, suggesting strip poker? Are he and Donny missed, or not at all? Did he see Geno's car flip sideways and disappear, like a small plane, over this curve. He saw something.

In his mind he is talking to a cop. "I saw the car swerve—yes, out of control—to the right. It was too far to the right. That's when he overcompensated. My goddamn brother. "

That's water. That's all black Matlacha Gulf of Mexico rocky bottom water, deep, rocky, and deep. That's what he's looking at.

Buck listens. He doesn't hear cars.

He thinks he can hear screams, but they don't make any sound. How is he going to rescue five people? Women first. Don't move people. Give CPR. His thinking—he is following his brain's agility.

You know what people will say? The wrong brother died. Buck starts crying, and he creeps down to the dock and calls into the blackness, the cool boards snagging his shirt, "Geno, brother, hello! Hello! Anyone!" His voice barks. He sounds army-strong. "Anyone!"

Where are the cars—he flails his arms around and sits back up, over his knees, and finds himself puking on the dock. And shaking. "No," he whispers. "No." It couldn't have happened. Geno would not lose control of his car, with folks in it, good folks.

Buck feels ridiculous, kneeling there in the night.

He thinks he sees the car out there on the navy blue water. But he doesn't. But he keeps thinking he does. He sees the dead bodies, the hair of Mim Satterwhite. But then he just sees flashes of water, not flesh, in the moon-bright. He thinks of Mim's ankles, in her white sandals, dancing between his feet, clicking like magnets, and her smell, gardenias and wine. He starts crying, because he can smell that smell now. He looks around for a bush, flowers to blame it on.

Buck runs back up to his car. He lets Donny sleep. He drives careful, fast, back to the Captain, kicks in the back door of the empty bar. But he is afraid to go in. He walks around the shack, out on the dock, surveys the sea again—feels time wasting like a tube, and then he runs into the place and uses the phone in the kitchen to call 911. Their unit, which is located in Matlacha, on the next island, toward the mainland, is forty-five minutes away.

"There's been a terrible accident. I think y'all need to get out here. It's right past where 237 cuts out to the bay. That curve. There's no guardrail, no nothing."

"We got it," the woman says. She sounds weak, bored, beautiful, like his daughter. He has tears streaming out of him, and he tries to keep tasting them, because he can feel that he is alive with that salt taste on his tongue.

When he gets back to the car, round front of the Captain's Bar, Donny is gone.

"Oh, for Pete's sake," Buck cries. He bangs the top of his Landau. He thinks about going back in for a drink, to wait where it is quiet and safe, inside the dark empty bar. "Donny!" He yells into the night.

The wheelchair is still poking out of his trunk—no fucking wonder it was so dark in the car—he couldn't see out of his back window with that piece of shit back there.

Buck rips the chair out of his trunk and, with an amazing amount of energy, flings it across the parking lot of Captain's. It lands sitting up, unfolding, like it has a life of its own, like it's going to take off on its own.

"Don! Donald! Donald!"

It seems likely and unlikely that Geno's car has beached, and everyone is safe, cold, wet, traumatized, but safe, huddled under blankets, with a fire and brandy.

"Donny!" he shouts. "Geno!" He looks around for Donny. "Don!"

"It's like losing a fucking elephant in a china shop." He shouts. Lights come on in the woods behind the bar. *That's Old Joe's,* he thinks. He wants to get people, roust them out, but he doesn't know, he doesn't know, what do you do, what do you tell them? My brother—people. Dead. I think.

Furious, he screeches down the road, back to the scene, where he could be of help.

He walks down to where in this world he was last sure—leaving his car in the middle of the road, with the emergency flashers on. Trying not to think about Donald—the fat asshole wouldn't try to off himself, would he? Buck is furious he has to worry about things like that at a time like this.

No one passes him; no cars come. He doesn't hear sirens.

A truck veers right up on him. Buck is on the wet rocks. He has a flashlight, but it isn't working. The sea is soaking him up to his knees. His legs are cold. He is still crying. Geno's wife isn't going to believe him. Donny isn't going to remember. A blond surfer sinewy kid bounds out of the truck, all awake.

"Does that look like the roof of a car; does that look like red metal? It's a red car—there could be survivors. I need a rope—"

"Buddy, old man, get the hell off that rock. Get up here. You're going to fall in."

It's some young punk yelling at him. Buck looks busy, real focused on the situation. "God, we need to get some help. I'm not fooling around. This is real bad. Look out, kid."

He keeps seeing the women, the hair floating, the bubble that the car is, he sees them with smiles on their faces, he cannot see the faces of the men—they do not exist. The women, they're still there. He can feel it. He can feel it, and he starts weeping. He lies down on the rock, and lets the water lap him like a sick sad tongue.

He feels for his wallet. Donny has perhaps stolen it. He had a lot of money tonight. At one point, he had a fat dry wallet and ten hundred dollars.

"Buddy," the kid says. "Hey, buddy. Get up here, man. Get up on the shoulder, you're going to go in the drink, dude."

Buck does not get up. The rock feels like a mattress for the gods, he thinks. What is happening to Geno at this moment, he wonders. He lolls his head back. There are dozens of oily-looking stars poking in the fabric of the night. The back of his head feels like it is bleeding now.

"I'm going for help, man." Then the truck takes off.

"Help would be good. Help would be real good. Glad you thought of that."

Buck waits there, for someone, or something, or the next hour, or some help to come from whatever direction it's going to come from.

Florida Law

My mother wouldn't let my father in our house. They struggled with the front door between them.

"Then goddamnit, hand me my suits and some underwear and the drill," he said, letting go of his side of the door so my mother got knocked hard on the forehead with that wave of wood. Behind Dad was a big-breasted, much taller woman in a white suit, a pale-eyed woman with large hair and white eyelids and a bright pearl choker. Not a lady friend we had seen on our porch before.

My mother yelled at me to get in my room, the same way she yelled when there were two dogs connected to each other in our front yard.

"Jesus," the pearl choker woman said.

I felt so bad. It wasn't fair that my father brought someone with him, to witness this, someone we were losing him to.

My mother stopped her scream and turned to give me her regular voice now, a soft-hard voice that you could almost see through, but you couldn't. "Georgia. Lock yourself in your room this instant. Move it."

The next morning I walked down the driveway by myself, in the same clothes, toward the bus stop. My father's shiny brown suits were all over our front yard like a pack of giant dogs had been by and messed. The suits looked slimy with dew on them. What do you tell yourself in times of great tragedy like this? *It isn't happening.*

I couldn't go to the bus stop. The Garamellas had already been past my crazy front yard. I could see their curly halos of hair down there at the corner already. I returned to the house quickly and had to knock and knock and yell at my mother to let me in. She was in tears.

My father had gotten married, she said.

How I sleep through these things I will never figure out.

My mother and I moved out; the new wife moved into our house. My mother and I weren't in our apartment two weeks (one of my father's not-so-great units, by the park behind my junior high school), and the big pearly woman, the new wife, came by our apartment to tell us how it was going in our old house.

"Let's try to behave like *adults*," the big pearly woman said to me through the little dirty marbled window in our apartment door. She didn't say "adults" like we did in our family. "Ad-olts," she said. Like we all were some kind of tiny machine parts that always got lost.

My mother wouldn't come out of the apartment's bathroom. My mother hadn't signed any papers and refused to condone or believe any divorce. She hadn't given any consent. She was Catholic, or had been a long time ago, and they didn't condone divorce under any circumstances except if one of the parents was brutally torturing one of the children.

But she didn't know everything.

That summer Florida had changed all its laws. We'd been studying Florida law in Civics before my mother moved us into the apartment and made me quit going to school. Government in the Sunshine, English-only, The Lemon Law, No Fault Insurance, and No Fault Divorce—I had read ahead in our book. Now, you could get what you wanted the way you wanted it, and you could unload anything you didn't. She didn't know. You could change the state bird from mockingbird way on over to parrot. You could buy pieces of the ocean, pie slices of water; you could own something moving like that, like water. Whatever had to do with bad cars and new wives you could do quite freely. I'd read ahead. You just had to do it in the sunshine so everyone could see.

Much worse laws, I thought. I kept my learning to myself. I figured it had to last me—who knew when she'd let me out of the apartment. Bad cars and new wives are the two things in life that should be kept as quiet as possible. I wanted to be in the dark desperately. Me and my mother stood half a chance only in the dark, an agreed-upon dark.

And here that woman was, at our door. I stood there in our apartment's doorway, covering that glass pane with my hands, trying to keep light and thereby the new wife from coming in. Even though the door was locked and chained, I still felt she could break it down. She was a huge couch of a woman. She had a break-this-door-down look in her eyes. I was looking at the balcony railing behind her instead of right at her, how it looked like wire. How hard this woman of my father's would fall onto the parking lot, but how impossible it would be to push such a sofa of a woman over the edge. She'd boink back up and kick me in the chin. I wanted to plant my hands on her breast cushions and push harder than I had ever pushed. But my mother had strictly forbidden opening the door under any circumstances.

"Let me talk to your mother, kid." She didn't yell. Loud and clear was her normal voice. Her fingernails had white polish that looked like gelatin, and her eyelids were frosty white, and she was pushing on the metal door of our apartment with those nails so that my teeth and the bones in my feet hurt like ice.

I pushed our door against her, and my father's bride, this enormous buxom woman, pushed back. It is the first most scary thing that has happened to me. My first violence. Even though there was a locked door between us, a door that was not moving or breaking, it was like she was trying to kill me. Why was she trying to come in? What was she doing here? My father wouldn't have wanted her to be doing this. You didn't shove the dumped-family's door. You sent them checks.

By shrieking in a high-pitched and sexual squeal I got rid of her. I could scream like my mother. It could be frightening. It took every-thing out of you. You had to say, okay, I am letting my entire self go. I am willing to die in this scream. I am willing to keep on screaming. I will scream until someone official arrives; it could be days or months. You have to give your all to it, until your entire self is gone, until all that's left of you is the scream.

She left. I ran around and closed the mangy green dingleball curtains, the same ones that had been in my room when I was baby, and I went to cry in the bathroom with my mother.

"I want to die," my mother whispered in her shuddering cry. For a second I thought she meant to have the woman come on in then. My mom was so tiny. She had her hair in pins, X's all over her tiny head. I was scared to touch her because she seemed so *sharp*, and I was scared not to touch her, not to cover her edges with my roundness.

We were scared of this woman. Had I let that woman in, my mother would have killed herself. The woman would have killed us. She didn't seem like a normal woman at all. It was getting to that kind of unreality. Nothing was far away from and nothing was close to happening.

I held my mother, but she wouldn't move. I knew if I dug my finger-nails into her skin to get her to stop turning gray, I would take a nick out of her. My mother was turning to wax. I felt my fingers press onto her cool skin, and we sat like that, scared on the edge of the tub, until late, late night.

The next day is the same: me on the toilet in my father's apartment complex, my mother shaking at my feet in the dry bathtub, and the wife banging on the metal door like she is hail.

"Ladies, open the goddamn door for Christ's sake!"

The woman could break the door down.

But each day, she roared off again and again in a rusty white Cadillac.

We didn't have a phone. I knew better than to send my father a letter—that would be intercepted. I watched her peel out, shooting our front window the finger, and I couldn't understand.

It didn't occur to me that stupefaction was the correct response. Disorder fit right in, blended with dinner and desire and the morning light.

"I'll make chili mac," I said when I came from the window back to the bathroom. I was always hungry. My mother wasn't eating at all. She was melting away. It made me feel guilty for being so hungry. I tried to keep a lot of air in my stomach just by breathing and holding it in. I tried to think of the boys I loved at school and missed so dearly. That made me less hungry, because it moved my feeling lower than my stomach.

My mother cried in the tub, large dry sobs, a dry tub.

"You eat, I can't." She was shrinking. "Could you turn the lights off?" She was curled up in the cracked bathtub, my mother, hollow, a gray husk, like a long-dead bug you'd find in the back of your best cabinet in a porcelain cup.

In our new life, in the apartment, hiding out, my mother was worried about the new wife breaking in and beating us up with her fists, but she was equally worried about my legs, my breasts, my vagina. She wouldn't even say the word *breast* out loud. She said I wasn't going to school until things settled down because my father would be trying to kidnap me, the bride to kill me.

He would want me, though. He would take her to court and sentence her unfit, but I think she was glad to keep me out of school because my breasts had come out. My breasts were now things that needed immediate attention. Like loose buttons on the front of me, they needed some kind of repair. To top it off, I had gotten my first period. That is another story and too weird to go into here. The centrifugal problem, that which all spun around, was that I had only been able to bring my backpack with me, we left so fast. All I had in it were two pair of panties, which I had to wash in the sink, my Math and Civics folders, and my love letters. She'd found my letters from Oscar Love and taken them to the tub with her. The one good thing I had, she had. The one thing I had to read, she was reading.

Oscar drew me in the margins. Usually with huge breasts labeled "the Georgian Torpedo Tits." I would also be on top of him, and he would be very well endowed and gorgeous, and our hair was long and curly and exactly the same, linking us like we were in a bed of mossy hair. He drew lies, but they were great. He wrote stories in a circle around the drawings. It all seemed shocking at first, but if you looked long enough, the love came through.

"Those letters," I said, leaning into the bathroom, holding onto the door so it swung me in, "were planted in my backpack by a retarded boy."

"Well, Georgia." My mother looked like she would stand up in the tub. "I am going to call all the people in the phone book named Love and have them over, one by one, for a serious discussion. With the evidence. As soon as I can. You watch, young lady. You think you are so smart. We will just see about that, miss. This is not one bit funny. I am going to prosecute this matter."

I figured attention would help Oscar's career as an airbrush artist, not hurt. So I wasn't scared, I wanted the letters not to get all messed up in the bathtub, even though it was a dry tub.

My mother cried all day and wouldn't talk to me about my father or the woman or my education or the drawings or my bra possibilities. I thought she could teach me some grammar or something flat and simple like that since she used to be a teacher, but she stayed in the bathroom all day.

"We could do the Palmer method," I said. That used to be one of her big things. Writing loops that connected in thin pencil. I sat on the toilet with shelf paper in my lap, waiting for her to open her eyes, but she only did if there was a noise outside. That woman. About to break in. A lot of noises sound like a new wife at the old door. She always seemed about to come back, to kill us.

"You need lined paper, Georgia."

"I could make lined paper."

"I heard a noise. Are the lights turned out?"

I crept, kind of sexy-like, to the front windows and watched the nursing home across the street go through its white meals and its white sleeping. I dreamed of marrying Oscar Love—I was fourteen now, but in some states you could get married at that age. We had just been studying all those laws in Civics. Kentucky was a go. But something made me think that the pearl choker woman was from Kentucky, and that she had been married at fourteen.

I did want Oscar on top of me. The more I was trapped in the apartment, the more I tried to hold my mother, prop her up in there with pillows, the more I wanted Oscar to get on me and squish all of this away.

Oscar Love had a motorcycle, and I thought I could propose a weekend elopement and he would take me up. His parents were hippies. I used to walk there with him, skipping out of school at lunch, and we'd sit at his mom's table and help paint leather purses.

"Hey, Ruby," he'd say. "My woman is hungry."

"Thank you," I'd say. "Thank you, Ruby."

"Try to stay in the lines more, Georgia. You are ruining some of the purses."

I didn't like that type of painting, but it was so neat to watch Ruby. Her birth control pills sat on the table. With her special mineral waters and her cigarettes. Oscar lit her cigarettes and kissed her, and they were like brother and sister. He was fifteen, and she was thirty. It was a real sweet way, I thought.

As long as I could get rid of my virginity first, I could marry this Love boy and then come back and finish up where I was needed. He'd asked about how many lovers I had had, and I'd said, please, get real. I was knocked up. At the time, I hadn't known what knocked up was. He was so impressed though. He wouldn't want me for his girlfriend if he knew I was a virgin. Ruby would die. I wanted his life, my own apartment, my own place to live, a different name. Georgia Love—it sounded like a seven-year pestilence. But I wrote it on the shelf paper over and over. I wanted a state with different laws. Sex. I wanted some self-confidence from the waist down.

This weighed on me as I watched the nursing home, trying to pretend it was a soap opera. But nothing happened. No one went into anyone else's pale green room. No one even moved their head in my direction. It was like a prison over there, but like a prison in heaven.

At night my mother came out of her dry tub and into the living room where I slept on the sofa. This was the old sofa we'd had in our house when I was a baby—now it was rental unit furniture. Many, many strangers had been on this sofa. Who knew what all had been done on it? Sex. Fighting. Bleeding, even. The green shag rug reflected on my mother's skin like the old cheese moon. She sat on the edge of the sofa, by my feet, not touching me. I wanted her to lie down on top of me and cry until she was done crying. Shriek herself into me. I'd get rid of it, that dusky shell. I would squeeze the true life back into her. Then we could get up. Walk down the street. Do something productive.

"Take care of your body, Georgia. It's all you have." My mother's words came out of her so hard I thought the sofa was going to tip over. It was the most itchy couch. I never noticed this until she sat on it. I don't know if I was with her in the tub or out of the tub because she came out when I went to bed, and she sat on the edge of my couch, curled over onto herself, like she was taking on the shape of the tub.

"I'm so allergic to this couch. I want to get my old bed." I wanted my mother away from me, but the minute she left I would feel guilty. This was my trouble: when I get what I want, I feel worse. I'm starting to want things that I don't want, like full frontal nudity, lipstick, to run away, and to take a lover on the secret side of the park behind us. When I get these things, I'll be able to see from a wider point of view, I think.

"It is not horsehair, Georgia. This is quality furniture." Her head bobs down onto her chest—she's a sleeping bird talking. "I don't appreciate you calling my good furniture horsehair. I just don't."

"Great. Fine. But I'm telling you, Mother, I am sleeping on wood and horse."

"You are fourteen years old, Georgia. Stop touching yourself and you won't itch. Listen to me. I'm your mother. You have to take care of your body." Her eyes are closed, and she is pushing down too much on my couch, my bed. "Don't make me fight you. I haven't got the energy." She melts out of the room, back into the bathroom where it is dark and damp.

We'd been hiding in the apartment for sixteen days and seventeen nights. I made notches on the back of my couch, on an exposed part of the fine wood. Low on Hormel tamales and chili and mac and bottled water and, worst of all, toilet paper—we'd come to the square-counting stage. But we didn't want to see the woman, the wife, so we didn't risk leaving. The wife left threatening notes on the door. "Stay away from him. Or else."

I saw her white Cadillac shimmering down our street every morning and every afternoon, but I didn't tell my mother. I was scared Mom would become worse. We hadn't seen my dad in a long time now, and I thought about sending him old Pearly Boob's notes at work so he had a chance to get out alive himself. But this seemed like an invitation to death. She'd tell him I wrote the notes. I knew how her mind worked—I was in junior high. He'd give her the keys to our place. Yesterday, knocking, her nails were longer and red, glued on, like in a nightmare.

My mother made cooed soft noises, about to come out of her tub for my nightly tuck in. Nowhere near sleepy, I floated on my couch in the dark, thinking about Oscar and boys at school that try to look like him—the Oscar wannabes. I missed them so much.

Thinking about that stuff made me hungry. This night, for some reason, I'd put my baby quilt into my pants, stuffed it into my underwear. I'd been thinking, how did it feel to wear a diaper? Why don't babies hate diapers? How do they get used to that ballast and padding? I wiggled, ground my hips. It felt so sexy, the diaper, in an oh-I-cannot-help-myself way. What was sex exactly?

I floated, puffed up on this stuffed butt, thinking those kinds of thoughts, trying to feel my actual vagina with my mind, wondering why you can't feel such an important place. Why they say "the walls of the vagina" when it seems to be nothing like walls. I don't know, but I think it is more like a stream, a thing that gets along with walls, but could take any form? I don't know. I haven't been down there myself. My mother says I cannot use tampons until I am married. So I've only seen pictures at school in Health, where there is a drawing in my book, which has been signed out to all boys before me. I would get the only

Health book signed out to eight years of boys before me. And bad ones: Ricky Husmuller and Andrew Snedeker, among others. Famous, condom-owning boys. They have drawn sperm and penises and teeth—and it is hard to tell what is going on in the blue part, the lines that lead out of the vagina and the uterus to the ovaries—it looks like a ram, but it is so hard to tell because it is blue and black under so much heavy boy-penciling. Figure 21.6 has been renamed "BITE IT, BABY." The effect of this book-uterus was of a devil screaming at you.

Maybe, I wondered, you feel it after you'd had a penis inside? The vagina comes to life, the walls figure their proper position. Maybe the penis rubs vagina-ness into the vagina. It's so hard to imagine.

The quilt bunched up in my underwear, and my panties were tight, real tight on me. Oscar Love and his funny little cousin who makes mukluks, and Ruby. What it would be like to move into a large house with them. What they would do to my breasts if they had hold of them. Ruby would make them grow. What would Oscar do to a nut knocking at my door. What would Ruby do to a nut knocking at her son's door? I writhed and pretended Oscar was making love to me.

My breasts were so small, my shirt was remaining on during sex, but the rest was all theirs, free range. No one will object. Because my enthusiasm and my vagina's delight will be so delicious to my lovers. If I was not a virgin, the woman, the new wife, wouldn't be able to scare us so badly.

If I were good at sex, experienced, doing it, I'd yell at her one-on-one. Maybe I could even get us back in our house. I'd punch her if I had the strength sex must give a woman. I could call lawyers. My mother wouldn't scare me by worrying so much about the vague fears she frenzies over my body. I would be brave and wise, able to quit school. Virgins can't really find work. How could you seriously interview for a job without your vagina defined, in position? I turned onto my stomach and hiked my fabulously sexed butt into the air and imagined *Oscar Oscar Oscar*.

This was when my mother came from the bathroom for my tuck-in. She sat on the couch—it nearly tipped—and I started itching like mad. I rolled over quick and pulled my sheets up over my body.

"Honey," she said, "should you go on ahead to school tomorrow?"

She wanted me to say no, for us to have our regular conversation— where I say I am scared, she is scared too, we should wait, handling my father is tricky, he might try to snatch me if I go there, we'd better wait until the dust settles, the woman will move out of our house, etc., it won't last much longer, my mother needs a few more days to build up some strength, etc., etc.

But she didn't finish her part of the spiel; she stopped and looked at me very strangely, her lips a straight line, like the quick kind a pen makes. I was all puffed up and wiggling. I had that quilt stuffed in my pants and was trying to slowly snake it out without her noticing.

"What are you doing?"

"Nothing." I eased the quilt out of my underwear bit by bit. It was bunched tight, and I had to go slow. It felt good. Is this what it was like when he took his penis out of you? I undulated a little. The davenport tried to buck like the pony that it was.

"What's going on under there. Georgia? What are you doing?"

My mother pulled at my sheets and I said, "Stop. Just stop."

I hit her on the arm, and then I hit her harder. "Stop. Nothing. Leave me alone. You are driving me nuts! Back off! I am going nuts in this place! Can't you leave me alone for five minutes?" I pulled the sheets tight to my neck and left the quilt a wreck under me and between my hot legs.

She leaned way over me, like a vulture. We fought over the covers at my neck. "You're trying to unpeel me!" I started laughing. My mother started crying. She got up, the sofa rocked back into the wall— everything made me think of *fucking*.

She didn't like secrets, mysterious movements under the covers.

"Mom," I said. "Come back in a minute, okay?"

"Why should I?"

It embarrassed me, and why should it? "I am sick and tired of being—"

"—oh yeah?"

Embarrassed, I wanted to say. If I could get rid of the virgin parts that made you wilt and go red.

The sirens blared past on their way to the hospital. We both stared at the curtains, though there was nothing to see. When it quieted back down, I sat up, still entangled in my sex project, and I said, "I was pretending to be a banana, you know? Like when we were little kids?"

She crossed her arms, hugging herself. "Listen to me. I've got one news flash for you, young lady. Take care of your body, Georgia, it's all you've got. I won't have you treating me this way. I love you. I am the only person who loves you, and I don't want you or need you doing this to me."

Suddenly she stomped up to me; I lay down, in a tight ball, like a baby armadillo. "Oh, I'm not a hitter." She was right in my face. Her hands pulled at the covers around my neck, but I didn't let her in. Her face sent off heat.

I never laughed since we left the house. I never laughed at my mother like this. But this night, I couldn't stop. Trying to uncover someone who is trying to stay covered up with one hand and pulling a quilt out of her body with the other—my mother working both her tiny hands at the blankets at my neck—it was too funny. And I couldn't get that quilt out of my pants. I was still humped up.

"I am the only one who loves you, Georgia." She flung me back onto the couch and stormed out and slammed the door to the front room. For once not the bathroom. She never went in the front room because it was by the street.

She didn't want to be seen.

I went out to the balcony with my quilt wrapped around my shoulders. It was so warm; it felt so good on me. I smiled at it for where it had been. It smelled like hay, a blend of the horse sofa and me.

It scared me that the woman, the wife, would come up the stairs. I got nervous with the door open for that long. I looked up at the stars and wondered. Which one is which. I didn't read ahead in that class.

At the time, I didn't know this was the reason my skin hurt all over, and my bones hurt, too. But I could feel the places she would bruise me, the small of my back, my cheek, my shins. She would kick me and then, literally, walk all over my mother, like my mother was a pile of leaves. I huddled there, under the stars, shuddering, wondering orgasm? or fear?

I wanted to dive down into it. The railing of the balcony was cold but the blue-black night air was so warm in October, in Florida, it felt as if it could hold you, all that wetness like a blanket of kisses.

By "I am the only one that loves you" my mother meant only one thing: don't have sex. She meant don't find your father. She thought of this as his big punishment—his new wife is nuts and *he doesn't know, only we do*.

The apartment was dark and creaking behind me. I breathed in a spooky cushion of that hideout air and willed myself wild.

"I will be wild," I whispered to the night. I felt very sophisticated and unusual for my age.

The walls were nothing like walls, but scarves of red air. I said to myself: I am here to unfurl. I thought about leaping over the edge, how that was the same as the scream that gets people away from you, my mom's scream.

The next morning I leave. I walk downstairs and meander all the way to school. I stink when I get there. It is far, and I only have clean panties, the rest is sickening. I am even getting sick of my one top, a sweatshirt of Oscar's. My mother would kill me if she knew that's what she had been looking at, his blue Styx sweatshirt. I'll be wearing it when I am a grandma, though.

I am an hour late, so I go into the office and ask if I can get a tardy slip. I keep thinking about where Oscar is—Building Three, upstairs, in typing, maybe writing me a letter? Mrs. Cudahey won't give me a slip. My file folder is on her desk. She picks it up. I see her nails are bitten, but she is wearing eye shadow. She smoothes her flowered dress and looks down at me. For a second, I think she can see. For a second I want to tell her.

"You sit," she says. Like I know nothing about Florida law.

Mrs. Cudahey goes right into the assistant principal's office and closes the door, firmly, even though it doesn't go all the way up to the top of the ceiling. I feel like they might be crying in there. My terrible life makes them so sad, they can't control themselves. They will never come out. It's tragedy. Nothing less can be done. I lean on the wooden railing by Mrs. Cudahey's desk, wondering why they put up these short wood fences in junior high school offices. I pluck my hand across the fence strips, hurting it really, in a trance.

"We were told you had transferred to Wisconsin with your mother, Georgia. Would you like to explain?"

"It didn't work out," I say. A completely Ruby kind of thing to say. "Can I call my dad?"

If Oscar were my husband, we could be together right now. I call my dad's office and he will not be in and they don't know anything else about his schedule. They are taking messages, and he has a pile of them.

"You will need to have your mother come in," Mrs. Cudahey says. "Are there legal issues involved, hon? What about your brother?"

This confuses me. This is a confrontation, and I am not ready. My brother is staying a year on Aunt Ruthie's farm, because he has extra energy and animals help with that.

Why have I left the apartment, the sofa, the nest? I forget about the law. I know if I get married I don't have to have my mother's signature. Everyone thinks I am nice and quiet and shy, which I am on the outside. They don't know about Oscar Love, or the drawings, or where I am in relation to my sexual parts, or what I know, how long it's been since I've talked to anyone, how scared I have been, what I haven't had, and how scared I have not been. People don't know our lives when they have them before their eyes, and they know nothing about these lives in the future. What is it you are supposed to say? Do you scream again? Would you think your life was dangerous? Do you make fake phone calls? What do you do? Would you hop the fence? Do you trip? Would you feel ready for blows, or both fists and kisses? What would *you* explain?

Myself
as a Delicious Peach

I was balancing on the curb, having sex. Pretending. In my mind, I was doing it.

Oh, baby, I said.

Even to me, *oh, baby* sounded ridiculous.

My dad was always late. My brother said they weren't visitation rights, they were visitation wrongs. My brother was having nothing to do with "el traitor." My mother sent me down to the corner for Dad to pick me up.

"I don't need the man in my driveway," she said. She was very against sex. She said things like *why buy the cow when the milk is free?* To that I said, Ma, I'm not a cow and I'm not wanting to be bought

135

anyway. "Oh, yes, I know all about it. Free love. Give me a *break*! Don't even think about pulling anything like that, Georgia."

She and Sid both harangued me about seeing Dad. "He's a loser," Sid said, which hurt my feelings. I thought he was trying, maybe, to be a good person. Or that he would try, when he could. I believed in him. "Honey, your father—" my mother trailed off. She was only fierce when telling me to not have sex. This world was vague; now that we were teenagers, she only had the first parts of the rest of the sentences.

I didn't care that they'd thrown in the towel on my father. I loved him. I loved everyone in my family. Equally. If I started getting down on one, like my mother, I tried to like the others a little less, so it balanced out.

I stood there, on my toes, leaning against the kumquat bush, bending into it, and pretending it was my husband. I had my eyes closed. Cars whipped by on the busy street. The day was hot and sticky. I was at a somewhat major Orlando intersection, Summerlin and Topaz; I felt invisible.

I wondered what would become of me. Who was I going to be?

I wanted a hundred men to see me naked so that I would get used to it and stop hating my pointed pink body. Squeezing my butt cheeks together, I pretended my husband was right there, *right there*. My body bent over, into the bushy tree. Waiting for my Pops, thinking of him pressing on me, pressing on me. Not him, as in my dad, but him, my husband.

My father pulled up on time. Shocking.

I'd been deep into it when he roared to a stop beside me. He didn't pull onto Topaz; cars swooped around him, horns blazing.

But my father was on time, which was so weird.

"Hi, Buck," I said. "Welcome to my world!" I was serious. I climbed in the car, yanking my underwear back discreetly into its place. I fastened my seat belt.

Gunning the Olds, my father was a face inscrutable behind giant green pilot's glasses; something was up. He hadn't looked at me, hadn't said hi.

The other two times he'd come for visitation, he was hours late. Once I'd fallen asleep on the curb, and the other time I had gone home and taken a bath that lasted to the next morning. I went to school a pickle, and he picked me up there, in Mythology 200, and took me to Steak and Shake for lunch at 9:30 in the morning. "Have ya done Leda and the Swan yet? Have ya done Hercules? Have ya done the two-headed dog? I loved him."

"Those were all 100-level myths," I said. "Can I have another strawberry shake?"

Dad was a busy guy. He had a lot of business interests. This was the year he was in pencils. Last year it was wine bottle holders. The year before, gold.

"Are you ready?" he said. We passed a car around the curve and sped past the lakes. My butt was sticking to the vinyl of his car seat.

"Born ready," I said. I hated the sound of my voice. My butt was still stinging. I felt caught, caught in the act. Settle down, I said to the lower half of me. I felt wet and juicy.

Whoa, girl.

I thought about sex all the time, and I didn't even know what it was, precisely.

But I was fourteen and thought I should sure know by now, every one else did, so I kept on thinking, *oh, push, push it to me, yes, I love you.*

"Why are you sticking your butt out like that? What's wrong?"

"I'm not," I said. I had it perched off to the side of me, trying to let the air conditioning whoosh up my legs, to my crotch, which I worried was abnormally damp.

We zoomed up onto the highway, past Lake Ivanhoe, all choppy and foamy and steamy in the hot June sun. Little boats, like letters from lovers. I thought that, *little boats like letters from lovers*, and felt I would be famous someday.

I smiled.

"How are you, baby, I missed you," he said. He gave me a slobbery kiss as he veered into the opposite lane; a truck's horn screamed. "Are you okay?" He squeezed my kneecap, hard; I hated that.

"I know you miss me."

"You're a snot," he said. "What do you mean you know. You don't know. I might not miss you at all."

"I know," I said. "I know that, too."

No way would I ask him where we were going.

In the backseat, I saw he had a suitcase. My mother would go out of her mind at that. Perhaps he was kidnapping me, one of those custody battles. Swipe the kid, white slavery, across state lines. She was always talking about that stuff.

"Cop," I said, as we passed by a black and white car on the freeway. "Is this the passing lane?"

"Confine your comments to the matters at hand," he said.

Confine your comments. Gotta love that shit, as Oscar, the boy I loved, would say.

"Remember," I said to my dad, who was drinking a highball as we sped along, "when we were walking through houses going up and I stepped on that snake?" I contorted so I could look up at the sky through the windshield, big blue pajamas with white splotches, so sweet. I opened my mouth and let the sun in.

"What?" he said.

"It's a beautiful day," I shouted, over the radio and the blasting-high air conditioning. "Where we going?"

"Classified. You're on a need-to-know basis, First Daughter. I have told you that time and time again."

"Oh, Daddy, I waited all week to see you!" I reached up and kissed him, as he was bringing his cigarette to his mouth. It burned my cheek.

"Ouch!" I shrieked. I rubbed my cheek. Would I have a scar?

I rolled down my window to let the smoke out, and he turned the radio louder. I rubbed spit on my cheek and watched it reddening in the sideview mirror as I tried to guess. The beach. His father's? JG's ranch down on Matlacha, the tawny island in the gulf where you couldn't swim because it was all *spiney*. Every goddamn thing on my grandfather's entire island was spiney. The boys, the sea, the food, the trees, the boats. There were tons of seaweed—it was not fun to swim. But we were flying down the highway the wrong way for Matlacha.

"Where are we going? Tell me, Daddy, I get to know these things. I am *along*!"

We had left Orlando and were now into Ocala.

"Where's your brother, what's going on this time, do you want to enlighten me? Why the hell doesn't he come? Do you have any insight into that situation?" My dad finished his drink at the end of that and put it on the floor between his feet. "I can't believe he killed three cats. Does he try to get out of weekends with his poor old daddy on purpose, do you think?"

"Well, you don't really like cats that much, Dad." I pulled my hair back into a ponytail, coiled it, and leaned into the rearview mirror to see what that did for my facial bone structure. Good things, as it turned out. It made me look eighteen. *Cheekbones,* I thought. *Blow job,* I thought. What the hell was a *blow job*? My father would know, but I wasn't asking him. At recess, I'd said I knew. I said I knew *blow job* and *suck off.*

I didn't have a clue. And I was already fourteen. It was pathetic.

"Gonna be a beautiful sunset," I said, laying my head down on his lap, sticking my feet out my open window. Felt so good. We flew along. I honked the horn, wondering who was I signaling, who was I scaring as the traffic whipped past us.

"Cut it out," he said, and he popped me on the nose.

It always hurt when he pinched and hit me.

My shoelaces snapped in the wind. "Sid's Sid," I said. "My brother is my brother. I know not what makes him tick." The bottom portion of my father's chin blinked at me, stubbly and red.

A weak chin, my mother always said.

I suddenly knew what she meant.

Once, years ago, we'd taken a road trip as a family, zipping up I-75, north over the spine of Florida, like this. We'd gone to Kentucky, before their divorce, our one and only official family vacation.

My mother'd slept in the car because she found my father's relatives, and their shacky houses, too dirty, too shacklike. The Clampitts, she said. Which I didn't understand; we didn't have a television. But later I found a cartoon book of the *Beverly Hillbillies*, and there were some apt comparisons: Zena Mae, my cousin, did fix us possum, which was fun to eat, because it was possum; and my Uncle Clarence did keep his money under his mattress.

Me, I slept on Aunt Stella Mae's floor on a pallet of old flowered wool blankets with Sid. In the middle of the night my cousin Dale appeared and kissed me, for a long time. I stayed very quiet. It felt good, and I thought about his lips and the cool fur above them every day for a long time. His tongue tasted like strawberries, but the roof of his mouth tasted like salt and wine. I thought I'd marry Dale. I thought about him the whole way back to Florida that trip, while my parents argued about taxes and whether or not my mother had ruined everything by sleeping in the car.

It was funny how road trips made you think even more about sex, more than you already thought.

•

North of Gainesville, we drove through a patch of rain, hard thunderous drops, a sheet of gray, for about seven seconds, then it was blazing sun again.

"Oh, Daddy," I said, "I am simply dying of thirst." Suddenly I had a Kentucky accent. "Parched, I am."

"What?" he said.

"Rest stop," I commanded.

"Oh, God," he said. "You have to wait. Come on. Really?" He said we were going to a great party, a convention, and we had to make time.

"I'm not packed," I said. "I can't go to a party!"

We sped into the late afternoon. He steered with his knee. His gin sparkled like crystals in his glass. He buzzed the radio around, looking for the game.

I slouched against the door, which wasn't locked, which drove my mother nuts—if you sat against an unlocked door in a car, she would fairly lose her mind. My father passed every single car, truck, motorcycle—we were flying up the highway. "You're doing eighty," I said. I was trying to say it neutral.

"You got the angle," he said. "It's not eighty."

Another time, Buck'd taken me to Daytona to watch the 500, only we didn't get tickets and ended up in a pink cement-block one-story motel on the beach, the Neptune Star, with a woman who had a son my age. He and I sat on the sand while my father and Ginger or Gretchen or Gretel took naps. She had a tiny German accent. The boy, whose name I forget, had a small dirt bike. I think it was Derry. Derry or Dusty.

After it got dark, we waded into the ocean. The little motel was dark behind us.

"Why you hikin' your dress up, because you think you're sexy?" he'd said, this boy my age.

I had thought he was about to kiss me. I felt sick to my stomach when he said that. I was burning, my face and palms red. "I was just saving it," I said.

The ocean crashed around our ankles. I don't remember who slept where that night, or if we even had dinner, or if I threw that dress—it was white gauze with beige embroidered trim around the skirt—in the Dumpster behind the Neptune Star.

"Please tell me," I begged. "Maybe I have brought the wrong stuff?"

"You're happier worrying than you are having a good time, that's the problem with you, Georgia. You are exactly like your mother."

"No," I said. "I thought we were going to your place. You know?"

"So what's the problem?"

I looked at my brown grocery bag, on the backseat, by his brown flagging suitcase. "Mother would never wear a bikini and I wear a string," I said.

"I would like silence." My father lurched us onto the shoulder, and at the same time, he curled himself off to the side and let out an enormous episode of gas, and then started cussing, and tears came to his eyes and the car smelled damp and doggy.

I kept my eyes on the road. I didn't know what was happening.

Horns blared, and he veered to the side of the road. The shoulder thundered beneath the wheels until we stopped, enveloped in the terrible smell of gas, skunk, and beer.

All I could think was, *I thought you wanted silence.*

He wouldn't sit back down. He remained hunched up over the seat, over the wheel, as we idled in the emergency lane.

"Goddamnit. Bum-fuck Egypt. This bullshit again. Goddamn it. Where's the nearest goddamn port-o-potty."

I stared straight ahead. I wished I hadn't been thinking of sex. I wished I was on the route to becoming a nun, a good person. Not this kind of person. The terrible smell filled the car, and I rolled down my window all the way. It smelled like diapers, inside and outside of the car. Where were we?

"What can I do?" I said, staring straight out the window, as though my gaze kept the windshield from imploding. I was holding the wheel, so was he.

I hoped the car would blow up—me standing, no sitting, no draped, in tatters, on the evening news; oh, the tragedy on I-75 continues to leave the beautiful young Georgia Jackson in shock—shot of me standing there by the burning car, my hair gold like Cinderella's, the car a pumpkin on fire, and my mother and Sid watching this, realizing how stupid they had been, how unkind, how selfish, how fearful, oh, their beautiful Georgia. She was perfect.

Till she blew up.

We were close to the Stop 'N' Go. But not that close. We were more askew on the exit ramp. The cars that passed us slowed down, and I waved them on. It did smell awful. Buck threw himself out of the car. There was a stain the shape of Africa on the seat. I wanted to touch it with my hand so I sat on my hands.

He walked around the front of the car and slid down into the ditch.

His beer had spilled. The empty tinkled out onto the pavement after him.

On the highway above, cars blazed by like rockets.

Quickly scooting around, I herded other bottles, the empties scattered round the pedals, and stuck them firmly, wedging them so they wouldn't roll, under my seat, in case a cop came up to help us out.

Then my father, who'd been into the ditch of weeds and rushes and back already—yelled at me to pop the trunk. He was back there, and I couldn't see him, for a long time. The sky started to get dark and bright purple, with peach stripes, like curtains being drawn. A flock of birds flew over in their sharp perfect V. What the hell were they? Geese? Gulls? Pelicans? I strained to see something I recognized, but they disappeared behind the brown pines at the edge of the highway.

A trucker yanked on his horn, long and low and then when Dad flung himself back into the car, he had a drink, a new one. A highball glass from my mother's good barware.

He was also naked from the waist down, his sport coat flapping at his thighs, and that whole dark weird business down there; my father had been standing in an emergency lane naked from the waist down, except for socks and shoes.

Naked.

"Whoa," I said. I looked away; it's what you do. I looked out my window. "Wow," I said. He was naked. He'd been standing out back of the car, taking his pants off. No wonder there'd been honking.

He slammed his door, and we jerked back into the traffic. He didn't agonize over merging like my mother did; he went for it. One thing you can say about my dad.

I wondered where the pants had got to. Where were the next ones coming from?

"Hotlanta! Hotlanta, here we come." He belted it out. "Hang on, baby!"

"Are you okay, Daddy?" We were near Macon before I spoke. "You want me to take the wheel awhile?" I was unsure exactly what had happened—sitting there with him, the bad smell, the accident itself. Things smelled like a hospital, and not a good hospital. I wondered if it was true a baby's diapers aren't stinky to the mother.

"I said Hotlanta, Georgie, did you hear me, Hotlanta, do you know what that is about, baby?"

"Of course," I said. I tried to smile. I patted him on the leg, but it was so bare, pale, and hairy. His suit jacket sort of covered the whole serious business frontal area, sort of not. I didn't care where we were going now, even though I wanted to.

He drained his drink, set it on the seat between us, in a nest of Kleenex, flashlights, a hammer, a *Hustler*, and a pouch of fish gravel. He grabbed my knee, squeezed it in the way I most hated.

"Okay?"

"Great," I said.

After a bit I said, "Should I call Mom?"

"Fuck off," he said.

"I know, I know." I banged my head into the dashboard. "We gotta stop anyway because I need a bathroom," I said. Mom thought she was getting me back tomorrow morning. She'd be calling his place. She'd be out of her mind with concern.

"Why didn't you go at the pit stop?"

"I needed a bathroom," I said. "Not a ditch."

"You kids are spoiled, you know that?"

"Yeah," I said, and I folded myself over, laid my head on my knees.

Right before we reached downtown—I could see the snarl of highways and signs and skyscrapers, all lit up and beautiful—he said for me to run in and get him a six-pack. I'd been sleeping. His hand was on my bare thigh. My skirt was pushed up.

"Well, I need a fucking six-pack." I woke up with his words in my ears like hairs.

"Yeah," I said. "Sure I can." The tears were coming, and I tried to think of sex so I would stop crying.

"Get yourself something, get me a sixer, and go ahead and get me a pig knuckle, too." The shack station was strung with all-colored Christmas lights. Two men were talking and wearing overalls. They had a deer strapped to the back of a giant red Ford. The deer didn't look awake, and it didn't look sleeping.

"Daddy," I said, taking the twenty. "I don't want to get a pig knuckle. They are so disgusting. I'll feel like a dip. I'll puke. I *will* get carsick and puke all over creation if there is the joint from a poor innocent porcine being in this vehicle. Pig knuckles are too weird."

"Oh, for God's sake. Just pluck out a good one, with the tongs. You don't have to touch it. Get a big one. Get one with a lot of gristle on it." He smiled. I don't think he liked them. I think he liked making me buy them.

"It's too gross," I whined. I went from looking at his white socks, to his sunglasses, which had thousands of me's, me looking worried and tiny and birdish. "Are you going to wait in the car?"

"Do you always ask so many questions?"

"Excuse me," I said, flouncing into the store.

"You're a Southerner, aren't you?" he shouted. The deer men were staring at us.

"Oh, hey," I said, but my throat was pretty closed up, and no words came out.

I tried to remember to wiggle my butt the whole way around the store, which is not all that easy to do when you are about to buy a pig knuckle, believe you me.

"Oh, boy," I sighed as I flung open the heavy glass door and grabbed his beer, the first one I saw. I hooked the plastic ring thing on my index finger and slung it over my shoulder and wiggled.

A knuckle jar sat by the cash register, the bones inside all pink and gleaming in their cloudy fluid. *They're freaking hooves,* I said under my breath. Two women in tube tops with two babies each on their hips were laughing. They weren't buying anything. They were standing there by the Cokes, laughing.

"Party time," the red-haired one said to me.

I looked out there—I had no idea if they could see his pale hairy thighs, the dark nest between his legs, the sports coat ending so soon.

"One of those," I said, pointing with my pinkie to the slimy floating knuckles. "And could you please direct me to the nearest rest room?" I paid and took my items into the bathroom, vowing to do it in the other order next time. A phone stood between the men's and ladies' rooms. Out back behind the shack, I stood there with my purchases, feeling damp, sticky, and dirty. If I called my mother, she would call the police, start driving to Atlanta herself.

The man who flung himself out of the men's room was a real good-looking guy, tan, curly hair down his neck, a broad lazy grin.

"Hey, sugar," he said. "What's up?" He stood in front of me, looking at the phone and my eyes. He smelled delicious, like spices.

"Hey," I said.

He stood there, and I wanted him to keep looking at me. He ruffled his hair, like he was getting out of the shower.

"Oh. Man. Look at you." He looked me up and down again. I felt skinny and cute, freckled, perfect. "Do what it takes to make it a good one, honey." He strode off.

It was like he was divorcing me when he hopped on his motorcycle without me.

Back in the car, I opened the Cheetos. The bag let out a huge popping gasp, and my father snatched it, resting his juicy knuckle on his bare naked leg.

"Here," I said. "You need a beer. God, that thing is dripping all over!"

I popped the top—they had been on sale—and handed it to him, sliding it across the seat so any police wouldn't see all this we had going.

"You could have gotten a quieter snack," he said. He flung the Cheetos into the backseat. You could smell the orange powder of them everywhere.

"Daddy. Cheetos?"

"They're driving me over the edge."

"Daddy, shouldn't you put some clothes on?" I flicked off the radio. He took a big suck off his knuckle.

"I messed myself, honey," he said. His eyes were damp, big. He was pushing the buttons on the radio, looking for a ball game, even though the sound was off. "You can get me a fresh set of duds at the next stop. I don't want to be stopping every goddamn minute—we want to make the banquet; there's a cocktail hour."

He explained about the convention, his old IRS buddies, how it worked, the dance, the sessions, the bag of goodies waiting for us in the hotel suite. It was a three-day party, and I would be his princess.

I saw herons, and gators in the drainage ditch by the side of the road. Lolling in the deep purple light. I wondered how long I could wade there before I got nipped. I wondered if people could tell I was still a virgin by looking at me. I put my feet on the dash and opened my legs to let the hot Georgia night on my thighs.

A trucker laid on his horn as he waddled past us.

"You could flash 'em," he said. He leaned forward over the wheel, and we sped up.

I thought about that. Wondered if that kind of thing might encourage my tits to grow. They weren't coming in. If they stayed as small as my mother's, I could see suicide, I could see dying in eleventh grade. I would give them that long. Then I was taking steps. I was not going through life flat as a board. Flat as a board, Sid always said.

Then about five minutes into the loop, he hauled off and whacked me across the face. Just out of the blue.

"Daddy!" I gulped, and then started coughing, and tears blurted out of my face.

"Goddamn Near Beer," he yelled. He threw the beer I'd bought into the backseat. He swerved, cars honked, the pig knuckle rolled onto the magazine on the front seat, and he leaned over me, steering with his bare knees, rolled down my window, reached into the backseat with the hand that had socked me. I was cringing into my door, sure it would fly open. He flung the entire six-pack out my window.

"Near Beer. No wonder I feel like shit," he said. "Goddamnit, honey, do you pay attention? What were you thinking?"

Underneath the hotel, we parked. The smells of fumes and rubber made my stomach swirl.

"You got any money on ya, honey?"

"I want to go back home, Dad. I'm just not wanting to do this. I don't feel well."

"I'm going to pretend you didn't say that, honey." He stood in the dim purple light of the parking garage and pulled his bathing suit on.

"You can have a good time without me."

"Honey, goddamnit, you're pushing the limit here." He was patting himself down, searching for the missing wallet. "This is your debut! Get up for it!"

"Daddy—"

"I want to show you a good time, honey. I don't do it enough. You're going to love Hotlanta; we're going to have a great night, a great weekend." In his suitcoat and tight green bathing suit, he yanked our luggage out of the trunk, and then he yanked me out.

"I'm going to go call Mom," I said.

"Oh for God's sake, don't even think about that."

"But I don't—" I wanted to be in my crazy mother's house, sitting on my bed, reading a long book. I wanted to be there, that's where I wanted to be. My own bed.

"Don't start pulling shit."

"Dad, do you even have your wallet? What about your wallet?"

"You are ready for a sugar daddy, aren't you. Geez. Future Home-wreckers of America." He lurched off, his white legs sticking out under the suitcases and suitcoat, his dress shoes damp, his hair like a wild patch of fire. He held the suitcase in front of his crotch. At least he did that.

Peachtree Plaza was the most beautiful hotel I had ever been in. It had an atrium. I knew this because there were peach plastic signs everywhere on stands, like butlers, saying in gold script: *Atrium*. The middle of the hotel was hollow and shot straight up to the sky, way up! Balconies wrapped around each floor, and I could see all the peach doors to all the rooms, story after story. It was like one of those Escher drawings Oscar liked so much. I could never see the appeal.

I followed my father, in his bathing suit and suitcoat, across the lobby. Fake peach trees, with gold peaches and pretend money dripping from them. Fancy parrots swarming around in cages suspended from ten stories above. Everyone seemed dressed up, even the plants, which had little white lights in their branches. I felt like I was on stage. Like I was making my debut. No one knew who I was. I could be anyone.

"Oh, paradise, here we be." Buck threw his hands back into the air, dropped his suitcase, and I picked it up. It was like I was in a movie, by myself, in a city, checking in.

Women were barelegged, sandaled, made up, dripping gold beads and hair-sprayed, feathered hair—big blonde women, every single one of them with great boobs. I stood by the fountain, where my father had planted me with his luggage. I had no luggage. I had been picked up for a pizza date with my dad and ended up in the middle of downtown Atlanta with water and conversations crashing around me, glass elevators making me dizzy, and giant birds whistling and fluttering around the atrium—and the Bee Gees cooing and hollering in their soft peach way.

"We're in Room 1212," he said when he returned. "My lucky room."

"You've been here?"

"Honey, I've been a lot of places." He brushed his damp hair back off his shiny forehead.

"Is this that auctioneers' convention?" I asked, pulling on my dad's sleeve, but carefully—if I pulled too hard perhaps his whole clothes would unravel, like a blanket or a sweater; one tug, and he'd be buck naked.

"Excuse, our floor," Dad said.

A clot of people exited, and I had a clear view of my father, who was lighting a cigarette. He looked like some kind of emu, those skinny hairless legs poking out of that big feathery body.

"Cute outfit," a man said to my dad. My dad laughed.

"We're really on the thirteenth floor, you know," he said when we got off.

"Then why does it say twelve?"

"Think about it," he said, and I followed him down the corridors, looking down into the atrium, where people glided about as if they were being filmed.

"I should call Mom," I said.

I pulled the phone into the giant bed with me and decided to use the Collect option.

I could imagine the kitchen—bare light bulb, Sid's Auto Traders covering the kitchen table, processed veal patties thawing in the sink.

The phone at my mom's rang and rang.

A loud explosion of noise came from the bathroom. My father groaned.

"Are you okay?" I said to the wall.

On the television was one long commercial for Li'l Peach Orchard, the hotel's gift shop. They had everything: mints, shoes, champagne, dresses, stuffed animals, golf clubs, cigars.

"It's awful quiet out there!" he yelled. "You didn't fall out the window, did you?"

I walked over to it and leaned out. I remembered Sid hanging from the balcony when we were little. "Oh, boy." I took a deep breath and let my body buzz with the thought of me falling through the air—would I be conscious as I went down? Who would find me? Would I linger for a few days? Would I fall like a dinner napkin, a kite, or a bird? Would I look beautiful?

I jumped on the bed. It was huge, the biggest bed I had ever seen. I flung myself at the phone and dialed the collect call to my mom's again.

My father flushed the toilet, and I was about to hang up when my mother said to the operator, "Calling collect? She's calling collect?"

"Do you accept the charges?"

"Honey, honey, this better be a terrible emergency."

My father still hadn't come out. More gas. I was going to have to take him to the doctor as soon as we got back to Florida. This was not normal. Accidents, and all this gas.

"What are you saying, Georgia? Honey, I am in the middle of sweeping out the garage—your brother brought another piece of car home—some kind of a chassis thing, he says—I can hardly hear you. Can I call you back? This is the most expensive way to call, honey. We've talked about this."

"Mom, he's got me in Atlanta. I don't know. I don't know what to do."

"Atlanta? What Atlanta. What exactly do you mean, Atlanta?"

"Atlanta, Georgia." I spelled out the words and was suddenly crying. I tried to think about sex. If I had a husband, how would I be acting? I would not be spelling.

"Oh, for crying out loud. What do you mean?"

"I don't know. Forget it."

"Well, you called. If you called, then I guess you should tell me what is going on. What's going on? What've you got yourself into?"

I was silent.

"What kind of tone of voice are you using with me, Georgia?"

I said nothing.

"Honey, you wanted to be with him. You made a decision. You have to live with the—"

"—stupid consequences, I know."

"If I come up there, you're going to have to be waiting out front of that hotel, Georgia. You can't pull a stunt like this; you can't keep doing this kind of thing. It's a *five-hour* drive!"

I held the phone away from my face and watched the television switch to a shot of the swimming pool.

My father came out of the bathroom, farting wildly, grinning.

A big, long silence surrounded us. I could feel the clicking of the phone—the money I was costing my mother. I tried to smile up at him. I could hear her sweet voice, chipping away, worrying.

"Who's that?" he barked. He was naked, with a small towel wrapped around his body.

How was I going to sleep in the same bed as my dad? Maybe we could order a bunch of extra pillows and make a berm down the middle. Like me and Sid used to do.

"Was that your mother?" He was reaching down now, trying to grab the phone. He had my hair in one hand, reaching for the phone with the other.

"No."

"How the hell is your mother?"

"I couldn't really reach her," I said.

And I was able to convince myself, somehow, that this was true.

At the reception, in the Golden Fruits ballroom, a huge cavernous plaza of a room, dripping with peach chandeliers, lined with mirrors, and dotted with waiters in black coats walking around with platters of champagne flutes, I pickpocketed my father.

Buck had made out my name tag, slapped it on my breast, which still stung, like a bruise. I hated myself, in my shorts, my T-shirt, my name tag that said, in my father's shaky down-slant hand, "Mrs. Jackson."

"Dad, it doesn't seem like we should be here," I said. That's when I slipped my hand into his back pocket; it was a joke. But when he didn't notice, I put the wallet in my pocket. "Dad," I said. "Did you hear me?"

My father ran into a woman in a slinky blue dress with butterflies made out of sequins. "Shit," she said.

A man in a green suitcoat and red pants boomed, slapping my dad on his back, "Ya hear the news? Shit like that?"

"Man. She was born to be fucked," he said.

The waiter guy went by, and my dad grabbed two champagnes. I reached for one, but he pulled his hands away. He hoisted the flutes into the air.

A cluster of women next to us, a cluster of men, burst into the tinkly laughter that I associated with fancy movies. All the women had boobs, and dresses, and there I was, like a boy or an animal or a ghost, my dad's wallet bulging out of my back shorts' pocket.

"You sure do like them young, Buck! Every year they're younger!"

"Marry me, honey, I'll treat you right, not like old Hoss here," a ruddy man with pinkish eyebrows said, leaning to me.

"I'll be back," I whispered up into my dad's ear. He smelled faintly of walnuts and grass.

"What are you talking about?" he said gruffly.

"I'll be right back," I said. I was stern.

"Ten minutes," he said, looking at his watch.

I smiled and curtsied and dashed through the throngs of dressy folks.

"Hey," one of the waiters said to me, and I didn't hear the rest. A warning, or an invitation?

I scattered myself down the spiral staircase, into the lobby. I pretended I was famous and alarmed, for a very important reason. Ten minutes, I thought. I headed for the elevators. I peeled off my name tag and threw it into the fountain, which had a monkey in a cage dancing around, right above the plumes of water. The letters melted off the tag, and it became a sticky piece of blank paper with a blue border, like a window, a window floating in the water.

Overhead, the parrots, who looked dressed up, seemed to think it was a good idea for me to go to the gift shop. To get some gum.

What I bought in the hotel gift shop and charged to our room was a purple wrap dress, out of silky stuff that wasn't real silk, "but acts just like the real," Marvelle the clerk said. It had a large parrot embroidered onto the hip, and it was a wrap dress, very low-cut and sexy. It tied at the shoulders and the waist. I liked all the strings. I liked feeling like a package, a present. In the gauze dress, I felt safer and gorgeous, both of those.

"Shall I bill to your room?" she asked, and that seemed the best way to go. I wore the dress out of there. I left my shorts and my shirt in the dressing room. I felt like a new woman. Marvelle had put blusher on my cheeks—it was actually lipstick, which she had also used on my eyelids. I felt quite flaming bright.

"I love to play, don't you?" she said. She had on lots of blue eye shadow.

"Mmm, sometimes, I guess," I said.

"There," she said. "Voilà! Now, that's a sight better. All right, honey, I got it. Room 1212. Don't forget your shorts! You don't live but once!"

She leaned over the glass counter and smacked me on the lips.

"Good luck!"

"You too!" I hollered and pretended I didn't hear her remind me about my shorts and sneakers. I minced along like a colt in the new silver plastic high heels, feeling vampy and stupid and brilliant all at once.

I stared at myself in the mirrors that lined one of the many posts in the lobby. All I could see was that I had no boobs, and this was a boob dress.

I took the elevator to the ballroom floor, and two men in tennis shirts and shorts got on. They smelled like leather, expensive. "Hello," they said. "Going up?"

I wondered how much a prostitute got paid, as I looked at each of them, looking at their faces, the skin there.

I pushed out my tits with all my might. Grow, damn things. Hurry up and grow before I give up and throw myself out a window.

"Have a good one, hon," they said when I got off.

I smiled back and tried to shake my hips, swivel them, the way I saw women walking, as I went into the party.

"What you got that shit all over your face for?" Buck said as we headed over to the bar at the back of the ballroom. "Wipe off that glop."

"What can I have to drink," I said, wiping my eyelids. I handed him his wallet. I didn't even know how much the bill was. I wondered what kind of time my mother was taking.

"A daiquiri for the Mrs. and a double Jack for me," he said. "Make that two of everything, would you?"

Well, maybe she would turn around and go back to Orlando; she had done that before. Miami, Matlacha, the Key West trip—she hadn't ever made it to any of those; she had turned around and gone back home. What I would do was, at 11:00 P.M., I'd run down and see if she was out there, and if I didn't see her in three minutes, no five minutes, if I didn't see her in exactly five minutes, I'd run back up to the party— at least then I would have tried. I would have done my part.

We stood in another line. My father was feeling my butt. I hated my purple slinky dress. What was I thinking?

We got oysters. I listened to one of his friends tell some long story about guys in New Orleans coming out of their graves and wanting dirt thrown on them. I had no idea. I watched my dad's ruddy face widening and shrinking with the story. The party was a lot louder than it had been half an hour ago.

My father made a big show of dropping the oysters down my throat. Everyone watched and laughed. I played trained seal, and ducked and bobbed in my purple wrap dress.

The oysters were so good, so slippery and salty and expensive-tasting. I loved their weirdness and ease. Until my father said, "Your goddamn tit is hanging out."

A woman tinkled up to me, with a beautiful cold porcelain face, a high forehead, and dyed hair. Her Indian bracelets chimed; she had coins on her sandals. I straightened up and wiped off some of the juice on my face.

"The kids are all out by the pool," she said.

I stared at her, dumb.

My dad slapped her on the back. "Open wide, Beej," he said.

"Okay," I said, and looked at my dad for a clue. I wondered what time it was. What I was going to do with the rest of my life.

The kids. *The kids.* Sounded so funny.

I keep telling myself I have to leave the ballroom. I want to leave my dad—he's being such a jerk. He doesn't stop talking or drinking. I keep telling myself: go check on your mother, see if she is there, just check. But I stand, frozen, unable to leave my father's side because I figure with me there, he is a teeny bit less of a jerk—it's so hard to leave him, to abandon him. It's so hard to make a move.

But finally, I walk down the stairs, and just take a quick look. I'm sure she won't be there.

I'm having a good look down the streets of Atlanta, out front of the sparkly hotel, when I see Mom's truck, the pea-green Datsun parked between two long white limos, like a lima bean.

She stands erect, like a military person, in a blocking stance. She has a yellow umbrella with her. She's in her uniform, her khaki jumpsuit, a kerchief over curlers. Why curlers?

I jump down from the planter, and she sees me, hustles over, all sturdy and concerned.

"What's your father doing, where?" She was vibrating. The bellman, with his gorgeous and perfect head, stands a foot away.

"Ma, I can't believe you made it." I take a real deep breath, put my arms around her. She sidesteps me. She actually points the umbrella at me, a teacher giving a long-overdue lesson.

"When my children call me, I am here. I do not like to see my children, either one of them, endangered. I'm here, Georgia. Like you asked. Where's your things? Where's your father? What's wrong? What the heck is going on?" She's squinting at me, and her lips are colorless, as if I'm causing her pain.

"Just wait here. Okay? I'll be back." I wanted to grab my stuff from the room and avoid any parent-parent contact. "I'll be back," I repeated. I put my hands up, like two stops.

"Georgia! You can't possibly go out into public in that outfit; that thing is falling off of you, and it hikes up. This is insanity."

I give her the double thumbs-up sign. "Everything's cool. Hang on a second."

"Can I help here?" the bellman says. I see his name is Jacques. His accent is soft and velvety.

"Have you had alcohol?" my mother says, loudly. She's still pointing at me with the umbrella. Hiking up my dress, I bolt across the pavement and into the lobby.

"Georgia!" My mother's voice gets all the parrots going, and they're saying, "Come back, y'all! Come back, y'all"

I dash faster and dive into the crowd, make my way to the escalators, and there she is, *right behind me.*

"Hey, Georgie-pie," Glover, one of my dad's friends says, grabbing my arm. He plants a wet kiss on my lips, slips me a little tongue. What a night, I am thinking. What a life.

"Your daddy said to tell you he's up in the room, and you are late and get your hiney up there." He winks and gives me a gentle shove back the way I came, which lands me into my mother's cold, tiny arms—like I've stuck myself on a tree's branches. Around us, the party continues, dancers waltz, swanky and sweet-smelling. I wish so much to be the girl dancing in the middle of the parquet floor to Frank Sinatra. But that's another girl, that's the not-me girl.

And there's my mom, her bony, cold hand on my elbow. She levels her eyes at Glover, who doesn't see her.

"Hello," she says, her voice steeled. She knows Glover from another life. "Georgia, gather your things."

I try to yank us toward the back elevators.

Glover is absorbed back into the crowd of suits and purple dresses. I feel like a wet parrot. The taste of that boy coats my tongue. Yet this chaos, these parents in the wrong city, and their daughter in the wrong clothes: it's a chaos laid out before me, and I have no choice but to walk through it, barefoot. Which I happen to be.

I press the peach disk with the umbrella. The full weight hits me. My poor mom. She doesn't do well in hotels. She doesn't get good results from strangers.

"Up? Why up? What? What now?"

"I gotta grab my stuff."

"You were supposed to be ready."

The elevator slips open.

"I can't ride in that. My fear of heights," she says. I put my arm around her. Press the buttons, and we wait.

"Why weren't you on the curb, waiting?" she says.

•

In Room 1212, my father and three other men, older men—white-haired, slack, shirtless—are all stretched out on the bed, our bed.

"Hey," I say. The door's open. We walk in.

My mom stands behind me, her face an afraid shade of gray.

"Buck," one of them says. But I don't know if he's referring to us.

I hear a woman's voice. I can't tell if it is coming from the bathroom or the television. I don't want my mother to hear this, or see this, but she's in. Like a sentry, all fierce and military in her khaki, her curlers like a helmet, too heavy for her papery face.

"Did you ever think Jesus committed suicide?" my father says. "He did." He speaks to the stale smoky air. The men watch television, eyes jelly. I feel like I'm in a morgue.

"Mom," I say, turning to her, "wait in the hall?" She isn't used to my dad. I have to protect her, to protect myself. She forgets what he is like. If she ever knew?

I move to stand by the television. They watch it intently. Each holds a plastic drink in his hands. My father sprawls in his bathing suit. The men are lying on my satchel, my wrinkled jacket, as if my things aren't on the bed. I look at what they are watching: it's like an animal program, with anemones? Or meat? Starfish, something pink and squishy. Then I see hair. Then I see a man's torso. And it's not the ocean; it's moaning, *oh, oh, oh, oh, yes, oh.* I have seen this all before, but it's so easy to pretend I haven't. I don't even know I am pretending. I feel ridiculous in the purple dress, a regular slink-fest.

"Dad," I say. "What are y'all doing?" I am afraid. I want to get my mom out of the room. More than anything. But I am frozen to the spot on the thick white carpet. I can't take my eyes off the man lying on my satchel now.

"Where've you been?" he asks, suddenly sitting up, coming to, taking a breath, ungluing. "I said ten minutes. You're a hell of a lot later than ten minutes. Where'd ya go?"

I think, did I make a pornographic movie and not know it? It's so weird, how guilty I feel, watching that slice of naked sex people. My head's filled, Jell-O-like. Seeing it, I am sure I'm at fault. Many things, my fault.

"Georgia," my mother hisses. "Please. I have to work tomorrow. Let's go." She leans against the door, propping it dramatically, sideways, with her leg. Suddenly the umbrella pops open. She doesn't try to close the umbrella. Instead she slings it over her shoulder.

"Daddy," I say. The room feels so tiny and hard. My mother glowers under her umbrella. All I can think is *Sound of Music* for some reason. The gazebo scene.

"Honey," he says. He is fumbling with the remote. One of the men stands up. I think I remember him from when I was a little girl. At another one of these conventions? I do not know. Some of these people came to our house for dinner when Sid and I were kids.

"Guess who is here," I say.

"Don't you knock?" he says. He is pointing the controls at the television, but it only gets louder. "BABY BABY BABY OH GOD COME INSIDE ME!"

"Wait out there, Mom."

"Mom," he says. "What?"

Should I donate my ugly bag, notebook, and jacket to the Fates? These men aren't budging.

"Jesus didn't fucking commit suicide." The thin older man sits up and glares at my mother, who hasn't moved. "Is she in or out?"

"Honey," my father says, still fumbling with the remote control, staring hard at the television, why won't it respond, and so I am staring at it, too.

It's not an animal show. Not at all. Did I still have hope it was? I see a penis, a huge penis, long, hairy, and dangling down, but stiff, too, and I can't believe it's that. That is a penis. I have a mouthwash desire.

I see now. These people are all at a pool party. They are all naked.
Their skin is yellowish in the light. There are women all around, groups
of people all massaging each other in harsh light, and the women all
have the breasts I want. Big. Loping. Sloping and loping. Breasts in
action. Breasts capable of doing things, of changing the way things are.

"What are you watching," I say, but I don't mean to ask.

"Where the hell have you been? I said."

"We're leaving now, Buck. I should think you could understand
that." My mother says this, from her post in the doorway, and the men
look at her. She puts down the umbrella and gently places her hands on
her head, to cover her curlers or to keep from screaming. She says icily,
"I'll be in the hall."

Has she seen what I've seen? What I've done? It feels real slow, but
the whole moment has been just that—maybe sixty seconds of me moving
toward the bed, and then away from the bed, and my things, and the men,
and my father. I haven't done anything. I haven't done anything wrong.

"Who needs refills?" the mustached man says. When he gets up, I
walk over to the bed—they could grab me—and I snag my jacket and
the flimsy tote bag.

"Your butt hangs out of that," my dad says.

They open the parts between her legs, and the camera moves in for
a close-up. Sea creatures, I think. In a way. I feel my stomach clench
and roll.

"Daddy," I say.

My dad comes over, stands between me and the television.

"I'm gonna go take a crap," he says, and he shuffles past me and
leaves by the other door. I hear my mother's voice out in the hallway.
"I can't wait very much longer. I'm about at the end of my rope."

"Oh, for God's sakes," Daddy says. On his way over to the
bathroom, he's seen her, in the hall, standing in a pool of soft light. "I
try to do something nice, look what happens. What the hell did you go

and call her for? Why do you ruin every single time we have together, baby? What's wrong with you? You're as crazy as she is. I'm going to take a crap." He lets out a lot of farting, and I hug him.

"I didn't!" I whisper. "I didn't do anything." I run to the door. He comes after me.

"Mom," I say. But I hope she doesn't hear me.

My face is burning.

"What? Why don't you both come in here and sit down and let's talk. Can we talk like goddamn adults? Then we can go down to the dance, as a family. Or what the fuckever you want. But stay here."

"Oh, Buck. Oh, Buck. You can tell this to the police. What is going on in here? Do you know your daughter has been drinking? Do know what she is doing? The kind of activities she is engaging in?"

"Mom," I shake her by the shoulders, and my father tries to put his arm around me, like we are friends. "Stop, Mom. Stop saying that stuff."

"Oh, you."

"What!"

"I can't believe this stunt you've pulled now."

We're in this tight group, just like the men sitting on the edge of the bed, leaning into the television. It's the closest my family has been in years and years. I want to push them both, so hard. Away from me.

"Why don't the two of you get the hell out of here and quit busting my chops. I'm on a business trip, I don't need the aggravation, I don't goddamn need it." My dad, it turns out, is holding an ashtray, which is fortunate, because his cigarette is all ash, a wand that is about to scatter into thousands of particles. I want to tap it with the umbrella. Instead what happens is he raises his hand, pretends like he is going to smash my mother's skull in. He snarls at her, like a mad dog.

"Oh, I wish you would," she says, and she is smiling, smiling hard. Wow, I think. She is crazy. Not us. I want my breasts to grow; I want not to be like her. I want my breasts to be huge. They are bigger than hers already. I want more, more, more differences. Why am I not brave enough to leave them, leave Room 1212, not ride back with crazy Mom, and find my own people, be by myself? Why am I so afraid to do that?

Then, Dad hurls the glass ashtray, into his room, past his friends. It hits the window above the television, and I see the glass slowly move into a web of frozen lines.

"That's enough, knock it off," the mustache guy says.

"Come on back in now, Buckster," the guy says. He doesn't look at us. "You were headed to the bathroom."

A woman in high heels is teetering up the hallway.

"Bye, Daddy," I say. His eyes don't focus. They are cloudy, and I have this feeling he doesn't know what is going on. Will he remember this?

I take my mother by the shoulders and steer her gently down the hall. She's rigid, like a praying mantis, but sending off that same *Don't smash me* messages, as mantises do. I don't want her to see that woman, all low-cut and busty and high heels and silver makeup. I don't want my mom seeing her knock on my dad's door.

I stay quiet, and we walk on past the jingling high-heeled rich woman. Of course she walks into Room 1212. We both look back. I think *oh no*, this is the turning-to-salt thing. The fancy woman knocks and walks in, one motion. I see the hem of her slinky dress slink in after her, a glimpse of sheer white fabric.

In the crowded elevator, my mother's hard as wire. She's breathing hard and ignoring me deeply and fully. I pretend I don't know her, right back. Staring out the glass, into the black and gold night of Atlanta and the city, stretched out like a sea with all those people going to all their normal and all their fucked-up lives, I think, okay. I get it.

I follow her, at a distance, out of the elevator, out in the lobby, and we leave the Peachtree. I think to myself, *Oh that beautiful child—she must be visiting from another country. Perhaps she is the queen's daughter;*

look at that beautiful hair, she could sell it. It's virgin hair, I bet. Look at it shine! Is she all by herself? That's what I'm thinking.

The bellman yells at my mother that she said she'd only be there a minute and it's been half an hour. Jacques is nowhere to be seen.

"Please, please, please, please, I beg of you," she says wearily, getting in. She unlocks my door, and she won't budge until she feels like it. We bounce off the limo behind us. The bellman shakes his fist.

"Where are your clothes? The tote is empty," she says. "What are you trying to pull? I don't understand you anymore."

"Mom, turn."

"What?"

"That was the turn for the highway. You never *understood* me. I really believe I was adopted."

"You are the least adopted person ever. Do you want me to show you my varicose veins?" She drives down a dark street, lined with warehouses. We don't know where we are going. It looks dangerous. Dark warehouses, people walking in the street, alone, men. No lights, nothing open. A pack of kids screams at us as we stop at a red light, and she checks the doors again.

"They're locked," I say.

"This is dangerous," she says.

"It's not," I say.

"You are on a very short leash," she says.

"Now, that sounds dangerous."

"I might run this light. I might," she says, jaw clenched. The umbrella is on the seat between us.

"Be my guest," I say. I'm so angry, I can taste blood in my throat.

At the railroad tracks, she has trouble getting the car to stay running. A long train roars by. I keep trying to think of what to say, what to talk about. I feel like I should thank her for coming to get me, but I can't.

When the train finally goes, she makes a big deal of checking for more trains, and then we finally cross the tracks, into this darker and even more desolate warehouse district.

"Can you see a street sign at least?" she barks.

"Forget I said anything."

I try to think: which is worse? Driving to Atlanta with my father? Driving back home from Atlanta with my mother? What if I had stayed? Would the men have been nicer if I'd been around?

She has trouble seeing the road, trouble with her clutch.

"You have to cover up. I can't stand it."

I do it. I put the worn windbreaker she has with her over my chest. She can't stand it that I am not wearing a bra.

"I have no breasts," I whisper. Sort of thinking she won't hear.

"That's not the point."

"Well, how could it not be?" But I don't want to fight her. I don't want to make her sad. I love her. I love her for showing up, ready to defend me.

"In fact," she says, after miles and miles, "I would consider your body to be developing overly."

"Oh, God," I say.

She tells me not to use language like that.

I stare out the window. We drive slowly, forty-five miles an hour, back across Georgia.

"It's a pretty night," I say.

"It really is," she says.

We get fried chicken at the Popeye's in Cairo. Then it gets light, all at once, at about 3:00 A.M. The sky is getting peach, already. It's amazing. I keep thinking about that woman, the shell between her legs. Why was she doing anything in the world like that? On television? What made men pretend to act as though it was beautiful? This monstrous shell between the legs. I was anxious to get home and examine mine in the bathroom mirror. I thought of my mother's. I thought of the woman's, the woman who had taken our place in 1212. I thought of the perfect linen girl's, the girl who would be a bride—what was between her legs? I couldn't imagine any of us had that in common. I couldn't imagine it was the same at all.

We eat the chicken in the car, trawling slowly home. After we are all cleaned up, with HandiWipes, and the chicken bones hidden underneath us, I start to breathe, and I don't feel so wet between my legs anymore. A little calmer. A little less of everything. But it's not until we are pulling into our driveway, slowly, slowly steering, stopping, that I have the courage to ask her.

What do you like about me best, I ask my mother. For real, I'm asking. What is your very favorite thing?

Sleep Creep Leap

Friday afternoon, on the way home from Atlantic Insurance, where she is the receptionist, and in charge of typing all Confidential memoranda, Mary Carolyn stops at the Shell station on the corner of Howell Branch and Venetian.

She needs gasoline.

Plus Gord Dort works there—has since about the time Buck left, five years ago—and Gord Dort personally services MC's vehicle, though he's a retiree running the register. He's not supposed to get his hands under the hoods, but she lets him do hers. A military man, a retired colonel who saw action in the Philippines, Gord Dort is always happy to see Mary Carolyn.

The day is hot and humid; cicadas buzz around her feet.

MC squeezes the handle repeatedly; the gas pump won't come on. She signals Gord, waving across the lanes and shaking the hose.

"Gord!" she mouths.

He's tottering slightly from side to side, behind his register, waving his short fat hand, beaming.

MC tries not to be annoyed. She wants to get home—Georgia's coming over tomorrow, and MC wants her to call, say what time.

She hopes Georgia will come early, so they have a whole full two days.

Finally, she walks into the store.

"Okay, okay, whoops, sorry 'bout that. I did the same stupid thing twice!" Gord's eyes are giant oysters behind his glasses. "Stupid!" He bangs himself on the head with both hands.

She smiles as fully and slowly as she can, which is extremely difficult because the sides of her head feel they will split open.

To regroup, MC eats a tuna on light rye. Then fertilizes the azaleas. The funnels she uses for fertilizing are of her own design. Then she turns the special irrigator she rigged up in the impatiens and sets to deadheading the bougies. She's propped the phone on the picnic table, its long cord snaking in through the jalousies. Every time she wheelbarrows past, she wills it to ring. *Call me, Georgia. Let me know you are okay.*

The phone rings.

"So can you pick me up?"

"Honey? Are you okay?"

"Hello?" Georgia fairly shouts. "Mom, listen. Listen. Can you come pick me up?" It's as though she's not paying attention to the very conversation she's having.

Mary Carolyn's heart clenches, the way the heart does when you are fifteen, and in love. It hurts. It's the future, sitting there in you.

Only now, it's her daughter, and MC feels heartbroken, in advance of any real disaster. She says, "I'll be on the corner in ten minutes."

"No. In two hours. Get me in two hours?"

"Now I'm just confused. Is your father—"

"Dynamite. Rock and roll," Georgia says. And Georgia hangs up.

The dial tone is weird, not your regular kind. It's lower, less urgent, careless. MC listens. It isn't even. What kind of phone, in what kind of place, is she calling from?

MC takes two pork chops out of the freezer and sticks them in the fridge. Georgia loves pound cake; MC takes one of the foil-wrapped bundles out of the freezer too and sets it on a little black metal rack, on the shimmering countertop.

Georgia isn't on the appointed corner, so Mary Carolyn circles. She tries to think. Have the visits gone better when Georgia has been on the corner of her father's apartment complex, ready?

Honking, then someone shouts at her.

"I'm doing the best I can!" she shouts.

Because she was going to work on the orchids, she isn't wearing her watch. Has she been waiting in her truck on this street half an hour? She looks in the rearview. Then scans all the black wrought-iron balconies, sticking out of the apartments like so many awful chins.

Georgia sounded so frantic. Mary Carolyn discovers she is grinding her teeth.

The stages of waiting, Mary Carolyn said aloud. "Worry, anger, boredom. Resentment? Confusion? I should write an article on The Stages of Waiting."

"Okay. Enough. This is it." She does one more lap, and then she heads for home.

Thus, MC's not really paying attention when she pulls in her driveway. She nearly hits the two small children standing at her garage door.

The small boy is waving a stick. It's the Pickett grandchildren—their mother, whose husband seems to have run off with their county commissioner, another man, if you can imagine that!—drops them off at Miriam's much too often. The children, who are still on tricycles—here are the trikes, parked on Mary Carolyn's lawn—run wild all day.

"Children!" Mary Carolyn says.

Her truck has stalled, because when she thought she'd run over them, she took her hands and feet off everything. She'd closed her eyes. She'd been given twenty years in the women's prison. Now, just as quickly, she puts it in gear, yanks on the emergency brake, and they come running over with their stick. Some clear plastic thing is hanging off the end.

When she gets out and inspects closer, it takes her awhile. She's on her knees in her driveway. The thing is being waved by the little boy—his name is Clayton or Caleb or Clifford or maybe Curtis. She can never remember. The girl, a year younger, who has never actually spoken in Mary Carolyn's presence, is known to her only as Sissy.

"Look what Sissy found," the boy says. He has a purple ring around his mouth, and his shirt has been buttoned wrong, so he looks bifurcated, like two halves of a person hastily stitched together. Sissy wears a Tweety Bird T-shirt, faded, and she's stretching it down to cover her shorts' front. MC supposes she has had an accident.

"Where, what?" Mary Carolyn is saying when she sees it for what it is. The item on the end of their stick, their proud find—it's a—oh dear. The tip on one end, the ring on the other. She's not sure if she's seen one before; surely she has. This one is yellowed; it's wrinkled and horrific and sticky.

"Oh, oh, dear." She grabs the stick from Caleb/Clayton, and his mouth drops open. It's bright purple inside that mouth.

"What'd you do that for?" The boy asks very nicely, after she's thrown the stick and its thing in the trash.

The little girl has tears in her eyes.

"Where did you find that? You are not in trouble. I just want to know. Not in my yard."

"Right here, in your backyard, under the sticker bush, right here," the boy says, marching to the spot. He kneels down and makes an X in the sand with his tiny index finger. "Ya see?" His eyes are watery blue blossoms. He looks like his father, the man who ran off with the man. What a legacy to leave, Mary Carolyn thinks.

"Just now?" Mary Carolyn says. She has the uneasy feeling her truck is rolling backward, out into the street. "Just now?"

"We never know when," the girl says, and she walks off, madlike.

Inside the dark, cool house, she dials Buck. No answer.

She puts the pound cake back in the freezer. The texture is going to be off.

She considers calling the police. Then she dials Oscar's mother's home. No answer. Then she looks up the number for Love Leather, where Oscar is usually working, and a young girl answers. "What can we do ya for?"

Mary Carolyn hangs up. In her mind the footage runs—Georgia, in way too short of shorts, one of her halters, her unkempt hair shining in the sun, walks across that park, taking a shortcut. Behind her father's building, the park is wild, and a ravine cuts the safe part off from the scary part. Georgia, paying no attention, scrambles down the slippery rocks, hops across the quick river, and starts up the other side. But before she gets onto the South Green, she's ambushed by the Winter Park stalker. Well, the Winter Park stalker was arrested four summers ago and then committed suicide in jail, in a closet where uniforms were kept. Someone like the Winter Park stalker. This new second-generation stalker grabs Georgia, who screams, but they are in the thicket, and he overpowers her. He has the advantage of surprise. She's wearing those dumb sandals with heels. He puts tape over her mouth, silver duct tape—

and here the movie jags to a halt and starts again—Georgia blithely walking down the outside stairs, three floors down, out of her father's building. And there is danger everywhere. And she doesn't know.

It's 9:00 P.M. The day has been a complete wash. MC goes out to her greenhouse and starts working on the *Phaius grandfloris*.

After an hour of cleaning the moss off pots, Mary Carolyn starts watering. She's thinking of Georgia the entire time. Worried, mad, afraid, annoyed. Having a daughter, to whom so many terrible things can happen, it's like being wrapped with wire straps and told to run for your life. She feels like she is spilling all over the place. She can't concentrate; she can't get anything done. Mary Carolyn stands back and surveys the orchids. They are so funny, such ugly things! She keeps them up because it bothers her to let things die. They were her husband's orchids. He asks her to bring them to him. But she never will do that. He has no room. He has a *lifestyle*.

Most of the *Vandas* are withered in back; the fronts of them thriving. It's normal.

She moves some things around, so the two plants in bloom are closer to the Visqueen door. These guys are draining way too fast.

She needs more sphagnum moss, so she leaves her greenhouse, walks across the driveway, and starts poking in her garage. A giant green citrus spider comes out of the bag of moss—once again, Mary Carolyn's heart clenches into a tiny tight ball—it hurts so much. She doesn't scream. She commands bravery to come up from the earth, through her legs, and to her head.

It doesn't. She darts over, keeping an eye on the giant spider—bigger than her palm, squeaky dull green skin, high elbows, and a sideways gait—as he makes his way across the pegboard; she grabs her Malathion spray contraption. She made it up. It's a system of hoses and spray and aerator. She uses it a lot. She should be wearing gloves and a mask, but there isn't time. She kneels down to his level, slings the gallon jug of spray over onto her back, and starts firing away.

This gets little Mr. Sphagnum-dweller moving. The spider, elbows high and specific, walks down the driveway. MC follows, low coating him with the milky fluid, so she doesn't even hear Oscar's car—she must have been so absorbed tracking the arachnid intruder.

The Nanner, as Oscar's car is called, by Oscar, nearly runs her down. My driveway, Mary Carolyn thinks, bracing herself on the rusty pocked hood of the hot "Nanner," has become a free-for-all for death!

She leans forward dramatically, glaring at him through the windshield. He's stopped not even an inch from her. Of course, there's Georgia, hanging all over him, and MC jumps back, drops her Malathion jug. The hoses stick out from her body; she feels like a poisonous hospital patient. Spray creeps down the driveway, thick white blood.

"You have to watch!" she says loudly. "I've been so worried."

Delayed and deliberate, Oscar shouts "Whoa!" He turns off the blasting radio. Music that sounds like garbage cans being hurled into traffic seems to be "in." Georgia meanwhile falls out of her side of the rusted yellow car, a Torino. Mary Carolyn is mentally taking an inventory of her own body—are all the pieces available? Within reach? When it feels safe, as though she won't be cruelly yanked from some part of herself trapped under the engine, she takes a step backward.

"Oscar, you—" she says.

"Mother!"

She hates when he calls her that. Oscar walks in his lunging froggy way, right up to her, making V signs—but it's not a *Victory*, it's some other thing—he's talking in some accent—she can't understand him at all.

Georgia, laughing, is all wound up in the kids' trikes. Is she on drugs? Sid has taught her how to look for the signs. The pupils are either too big or two small. Mary Carolyn wants to pick up Georgia's arms, look at the undersides of them, like you would with a plant showing early signs of spotty molds.

White stick-on letters march across the top of Oscar's windshield now. Georgia is dragging a brown paper bag—her things—out of the backseat.

She reads the windshield. C H A O S.

"So the Nanner has a new name, I see. Quite appropriate, it seems." Neither child responds.

In the hazy early moonlight, Georgia and Oscar look fleeting. Oscar's unusual looking and has the poorest sense of what might look flattering on him. He's got weirdly pale skin—Georgia needs less sun, the boy needs more. His dark hair is wispy, but coarse. There aren't many hairs, they're too long, and they're wiry. It's sad. But then he goes and wears huge mutton chops, way down on the face in a most lambchoppy pattern. A grizzled asymmetrical attempt at a mustache rides on his lip, and he has watery blue eyes, expressionless. Tonight he's in his usual thin-knit, worn-nearly-transparent shirt with thick long-pointed collars, and you can see the stays, those white plastic arrows, in the collar—they stand and corral the neck in an unseemly awkward way, too thick at the top, these shirts, too weightless all the way through. They make the neck seem stiff, and the body worthless. Dark hair, very no-color shirt, and pale skin—he doesn't look good with Georgia.

A dozen squirrel tails flag up the antenna: another new touch. Focus on the positive, MC tells herself.

"Children," she says. "You're here."

Now, running like an elf, with hugely exaggerated knees, *boing, boing, boing,* a giant hairy elf, Oscar yanks a rose off her good Kennedy plant and galumphing back in the same manner, he hands it to MC with a colorful swagger. He's down on bended knee.

"Not that," she says. "Those are—"

"We have news, Mother," he says. She has no choice but to gingerly take a piece of her plant he's brutally attacked.

"News?"

"Don't say anything, Ma." Georgia is wearing a scarf as a skirt. It could be called a pareo if there was more scarf available for her curvy hips. MC hopes she has a bathing suit on underneath, at least. Her bosom is too large for the halter she's chosen. If MC had had to describe her to the police, they would have had a very good idea of what Georgia Jackson looks like. The paisley kerchief over her head is new; she's barefoot, holding her brown paper bag on one hip, running one of the trikes with her other leg, her foot on the seat of it, back and forth.

"Honey," MC says during this silent moment. "I came for you. I was at the corner. What happened?"

"Oh, shit!" Georgia says. "I need a dress." Georgia leans against Oscar, and talks plaintively. "So, we have to get an early start, okay? There are three malls we can go to. We can go to all three."

"I tried to take her, but she was not very well-behaved!" Oscar pretends to chase and spank Georgia.

Mary Carolyn picks up the trikes, tries to ignore them. Georgia's thighs, her cleavage, her body is practically steaming! MC turns on the hose, half a mind to squirt the two of them down like cats or dogs when they get out of control. She hoses down the spray.

"I thought we weren't 'prom people.'"

"Stop now!" Georgia shouts, batting him, and simultaneously kissing his neck.

"Well," MC says. She has no idea what to do. She feels like she's crashing a personal life, walking in on something she shouldn't be seeing. It's her daughter! It's her yard!

When she'd had Sid, at some point, she realized how unusual and amazing it was to have a creature, not your sex, a thing with a penis, come out of your body. It had been with her for months, the idea of this penis coming out of her own self. But now, what seemed exotic and impossible was that Georgia, lush thighs, her giant breasts, had come from her. No one in Mary Carolyn's family had this body. So it seemed as though Sid, even with the boyness of him, was closer to her. This Georgia—her yellow hair, her freckles, her long legs, her thick lips— she was a rogue, a volunteer.

"Are we getting bitten up?" MC said, slapping at what might have been a mosquito, biting through her khakis. "Georgia, go in?" MC's thinking over what the garden books say about volunteers. Yank 'em up, or let 'em go; see what happens.

Starting CHAOS's engine is a large, lengthy production. It evidently has to "warm up." MC feels antsy, waiting for this to transpire.

She says to Georgia, because Georgia is thrusting the bag at her, and she already has the damaged rose stem, "I wasn't expecting you. I mean it's wonderful you are here, but I was supposed to be getting you in the morning, and then earlier?"

"Sorry," she says, but she isn't. Georgia leans way into the boy's car and plants an enormously bold kiss on Oscar's dark beard. Her pink scarf-clad bottom pokes way up, and out, like a risqué cartoon.

The stem is ragged; the plant wound will have to be staved and painted and plugged; that whole side of the bush won't flower again for three years. If it doesn't get infected, that is. She feels bad for staring over at the plant, but she has to; she's willing it not to get a disease between now and tomorrow when she can tend it.

Georgia is waving wildly to the Osc-man.

And he peels out, CHAOS creasing her fescue, where it is newly planted. The squirrel tails stick straight back in the wind—he probably loves that aspect, and then they whip around, as he does, zooming off.

Georgia is different, crabby, younger, sultry, and sulky.

MC, hands full, imagines lopping their heads off—so new ones would sprout, cleaner, healthier heads, and that thought allows her to smile and say, "Let me make us some nice dinner."

"Okay, I'm a vegetarian, you know."

The phone again. MC can hear it. They both run into the house.

"It's probably your father—why don't you get it?" MC calls to Georgia.

Georgia keeps walking, through the kitchen, down the hall.

"Hello," a deep funny voice says. "Mary Carolyn Jackson, this is Gord Dort. Gord Dort from down the Shell station. Will you be coming in tomorrow? It's Gord calling."

"Ah," MC says. "Oh." Her breath is down by her liver. She conjures some air and makes an unfortunate sucking sound.

"Who is it?" Georgia shouts from the hallway. "Who is it?"

Mary Carolyn hunkers over the phone. Why does she feel like she's about to be caught doing something? She finds herself whispering. "Gord, I don't know. I am in the middle of things here. It's not a good time for me to talk. Perhaps I could call you within the next few days?" She doesn't want to encourage him calling, at dinnertime, at home.

Georgia turns on the shower, then the radio. She changes the station from NPR to WDIZ; MC recognizes it from Sid.

"Tramps like us," Georgia sings. She cannot sing at all. "Baby we were BORN TO RUN."

She hasn't shut the door to the bathroom. MC imagines her standing there in front of the window, bare naked, advertising to the world.

"What's for dinner?" Georgia hollers. MC can feel it. Water is splashing everywhere.

"Pork chops," MC says. She's on her hands and knees wiping around the tub and laying down fresh towels. "But don't you worry. I'll make you a big salad and some—"

"I love pork chops! That's not a meat."

"It's a meat."

"Are you doing them with the bacon and the tomatoes and onions on top with the baby toothpicks, that fifties way? I *love* that!"

"Are you washing, honey?" MC doesn't hear any activity. The child is standing under the hot water—just standing there—it's probably costing four dollars. "I'm making enough for you. You can have what you want, hon. But pork is a meat. But you don't have to be a strict vegetarian."

She makes a cup of coffee and then looks at the clock—it's 11:00 P.M.! She thinks she should call Buck to let him know Georgia is safe and sound, but it is so late. If a woman answers, MC knows she won't sleep well. So she doesn't. He can call if he needs to know where the girl is.

Then she picks up the phone, dials Buck's number, lets it ring just once. It's her signal. She wishes they had a signal.

MC brushes her teeth, does her stretches, and wipes, under her nightgown, the fronts and backs of her legs with a cool damp washcloth. She brushes her hair—it is always at its best at night, just before she goes to bed. It's the most frustrating thing. She admires the hair, her favorite feature. A thick brown chestnut crown. A lot of gray, but not noticeable unless you focus on it. She focuses on brown. Her forehead looks high and brilliant; her blue eyes look stable and concerned. This is exactly how Mary Carolyn likes to look. Then, she puts on her robe and slippers, and turns off all the lights, and locks the doors, and hits the buzzer on the garage door.

Padding softly down the hallway to check on Georgia, she feels twenty years younger, full-breasted, happy as when the children were small, like Caleb and the Sissy person—so cute and earnest and even more so in sleep.

In Georgia's room, MC sits on the side of the bed. Then her eyes adjust, and she has a little unwelcome surprise. On top of the covers, Georgia is sleeping naked, of course. It's so shocking in its strangeness, her body, her round rump, the drapes wide open, the moonlight on her strong sturdy back. Georgia's skin is mottled—a month ago Oscar had taped her, crisscrossing her back so she could get a plaid tan. At least this was the story. MC didn't want to know. Georgia's brother, Sid, had liked the idea but deemed its execution unsuccessful. It had been that long since they'd all three shared a meal. MC had never known anyone who wanted plaid patterns on their skin, but if it was the worst thing the girl came up with, MC could handle it. Georgia rolled over, and MC saw her front had been taped too. Breasts, and all.

"Oh, honey," she whispered.

MC gets a blanket out of the bottom dresser drawer—it's Georgia's good quilt, from her aunt, Aunt Ruthie, and she fluffs it over the body of the girl.

She sits back on the bed and leans over and smells her. She smells her feet—Georgia didn't use the soap. She smells her child's stomach region, her nose less than inch, grazing the blanket. She's smelling, through the blanket, for evidence of Oscar. All she can smell is cedar from the blanket drawer. The condom on the stick pops into her head, and she pops it back out.

Her yellow hair is in the moonlight, as if Georgia had staged the scene to enhance her beauty. Her arms are behind her head, and her mouth is open, her lips damp. MC is alarmed, delighted, and feeling very old and withered. The child is so lush, you could plant things on her skin. MC leans her face down into her daughter's hair.

Cinnamon, grass, oil. Musk. Horse, cucumber—these are the smells of the sleeping Georgia. Unbrushed teeth.

MC puts her cheek down on the pillow, balances her coffee on Georgia's hip. Facing her, she watches Georgia breathe.

Her face is broken out, but in the moonlight, the bumps aren't flaws, just face, just skin, just Georgia, irregular and gorgeous and moonscape-like. Her bottom lip, symmetrical, full, almost Italian. The top one, nearly heart-shaped, had a tiny crease in it, like a cut, on the left side. It would hurt to eat potato chips with that. MC tries to think if Oscar wears braces. She looks for other marks and scars, examines the child's neck, moving the fall of hair to the other pillow.

Georgia moans, and her hands come down, and MC rolls back, holding her breath, while Georgia turns. The coffee's safe; quilt, safe. Georgia's hands disappear into each other, into her lap. If you could call it a lap when someone is lying on her side.

On her way out of the room, MC bends down to pick up the book on the floor, set it on the dresser. But as soon as she has it in her hand, she knows what it is, and she knows she's taking it. She feels awful, and as though she has no choice.

MC sits out in the hallway, the door to Georgia's room closed behind her, just to.

She reads only the last entry. Her coffee has gone cold.

Georgia didn't date her entries. At that age, MC supposes, one could remember when each thing happened.

The last entry is a list of boys' names. Mark Bledsoe. Steve B. Steve Cor. MC doesn't recognize anyone. Paul Thomas, Gary Self, S.J., Kent S. And on the facing page, the left side of the diary, a list of book titles. Georgia couldn't have read books like *Mansfield Park* and *Madame Bovary*. MC hasn't even read those. She intends to. When she has the time.

She fans through the pages. There's a poorly executed drawing of a palm tree. Oscar's name, or an "O" on many pages.

Then she sees, in large cursive, the only thing on a page, *Well. I am not a virgin anymore.*

I know a virgin; MC wants to find a way it could say that. She stands up fast, and her lower back seizes. Her head throbs, as though the coffee had been tainted. It spills; she slips back into the room. Georgia is snoring; she's broken out of the blanket. MC sets the book, exactly as it had been.

She went and got paper towels for the coffee-stained carpet.

Then she got in bed.

She couldn't stand it anymore; she went back into the room and covered Georgia again.

"What, what," Georgia says, batting at her, furrowing fiercely.

"Shh." MC feels as if even in the dark, her daughter sees completely through her.

On their way out the driveway, to the mall, it begins to rain.

"Well, we will stop at the Shell, top off the tank, and Mr. Dort can check the wipers."

"Oh, Mother."

When she and Mr. Dort return with the wiper blades, Georgia is all scrunched up across the front seat and peculiar.

"Hey, girl," Dort says.

Georgia will not speak to him.

MC drives, jaw set, pretending secretly that she is taking the child to the county dump and leaving her there. Georgia's resourceful. She can make a little hovel out of the discarded dressers and barrels, and she can eat all the wonderful grassy vegetables....

The fifth store is Burdines.

It is not a store you feel comfortable in. It's pricey, and swanky, snooty. Actually, MC cannot stand the store. She's never bought anything here.

"Look at this," MC says, holding up a leopard-print purse on a sale table. "Can you believe?"

"Frightening," Georgia says, sarcastically.

MC thinks of another book she should write. She wishes she had a pen. She digs in her purse, discreetly, while Georgia flicks through dresses on a tall rounder; *$99.99 and less,* the sign says. MC focuses on remembering the title for her book project: *Living Your Own Life.*

Georgia comes rushing up, in a huge flurry, with enormous mounds of dresses heaped over both her arms. "Mother, *what* are you doing?"

"Oh," Mary Carolyn says. "You knocked the wind out of me." She rubs her eyes. The back of her head is tight, as though screws have been laid into the nape of her neck.

"These, these, these—I love all of these. Why can't I have a dozen dresses! I would wear these to school—it could be so cool." Georgia twirls.

"I'll follow you."

Georgia prances along, humming and skipping to the dressing rooms. She reminds MC of an exposed, bare root ball. Need to get this one grounded, in the ground, soon.

"Is your father paying? For this prom dress? Will you wear it more than once, do you think? Georgia?"

"Mom! Let's have fun!" Georgia pushes Mary Carolyn into the tiny room.

Before Mary Carolyn can close her eyes, Georgia has stripped off her clothes, her halter, her shorts; she wears nothing under these.

MC thinks she will fall over. The front of her head starts hurting. It's like it's speckled with painful tiny wicks. Inside and outside her brain, wicks of frizzly fire.

"Can you stand this one? Oh my God!"

"Honey, please don't say—"

"Look, oh man, Oscar will completely and thoroughly die."

"Well, that wouldn't be the worst thing."

Naked again—she's like a snake. Georgia waggles her breasts up at the ceiling, does the lascivious tongue thing, and rolls her eyes and shoulders.

"I'm waiting in Shoes. You'll find me in Shoes."

Mary Carolyn gets her breath there.

The child's breasts are so big. Her father's side.

•

They don't leave the mall with a dress, and Mary Carolyn feels it is her fault. It's four in the afternoon. She wanted to repot the purple *vandas* and then set to scraping peeling paint off the west side of the house; that's not going to help. In addition to feeling annoyed with and sorry for Georgia, she's mad, mad at her daughter, mad at herself.

Georgia is pressed up against the glass window, pouting, and MC doesn't blame her.

MC bites her tongue. She doesn't ask her burning question. Nor does she ask, "When did you and Oscar become prom people, exactly?"

At home, Georgia goes to the phone, has a hushed call, then she's in the shower, standing in there, singing something but not with the tune.

MC takes an aspirin. Her skull feels pressed between rough boards.

"Honey, I'm going to lie down for fifteen minutes. Okay?"

Georgia doesn't answer. The door to her bedroom is closed.

Mary Carolyn figures she is writing nasty things about how horrible her mother is.

The light.

She can't get rid of the light. She closes the drapes and ties a black silk scarf around her eyes, but it hurts, and the room is still so light. It's a milky, wavering light, like when you lie on the bottom of a lake and look up. It makes Mary Carolyn dizzy to close her eyes and nauseated to open them.

She is in her bed.

She is both hot and cold.

Her head's a frozen fire.

She tries to watch the pain. She tries to breathe into the corners of the pain, as she has been taught, but it's stupid and impossible.

She breathes carefully. If she disturbs her cheeks, anything, her nostrils, if they move, she is racked with pain.

Her neck is like a thick cable of rigid wire.

She thinks she hears Georgia sobbing in the bedroom. But she can't move—zickety Z's are vibrating on the sides of her eyes, and the ceiling has turned blue.

When she gets up, it is dark.

She hasn't slept, but she hasn't been awake either. She feels drained of all her energy, but not stressed about the money, the dresses. She wants to make them dinner.

She goes to the kitchen and gets out the ground beef. She cuts the peppers in half and blanches them. She turns on the radio, but it's too loud, scratchy, and static, so she is fiddling with the record player, trying to get the arm to not keep jolting over the entire record in this way—it's like her windshield wipers. Sibelius. That music feels fine.

She calls Georgia. "Do you want to come set the table?"

No answer.

She keeps thinking she sees a condom out of the corner of her eye, but it's the streetlight, a blossom, a piece of Saran.

The beef smells delicious, and she realizes how hungry she is. She knocks softly on the bathroom door.

"Honey?"

On the counter, Georgia's makeup is scattered all over, like a crazy painter's been there.

In Georgia's cool dark room, MC pats the covers. She barely whispers. Her stomach is full of seams. She's so afraid. So many bad things. *Honey, I've started dinner. You want to set the table?* She wants Georgia to come out and talk to her. She feels she has lost her, ruined her.

Honey.

The covers aren't right.

The covers are covering pillows.

Georgia is gone.

MC bursts into tears.

•

The next morning, she hears a car in the driveway. At first she thinks it's Buck. She looks out the window. It's a shorter man, a shrub of a man.

Gord? MC is aghast. She opens Sid's window, to let air in. She whispers out into the morning. "Gord!" She does her best surprised face. She is supposed to be aghast. She has no idea what she feels—except that she doesn't want this to be happening; she feels denuded. Like a plant, stripped of its leaves, its flowers, its very stems, a bare wire coming out of the ground.

He's holding a dozen roses, in his bare hands, and he is not wearing gloves.

The remnants of the migraine are there, like scum on a pot—it's there. If she should try to stand on her head, for example, it would come back with a vengeance.

"My!" she says. She is fully dressed; she goes out to the driveway.

"Well," he says. He doesn't offer the flowers. He stands there. His hair is planked down close to his head, and she smells the Old Spice. He is in a pink guyabera, and shiny black shoes.

He clears his throat. There's a lot of phlegm. "It could be a companionship marriage. I heard about this on *Oprah*. Not a show I watch, but it's always on at the station, you know."

MC can't think of a thing to say. His shirt needs ironing. But it seems easier to have gotten in his car than to deal with inviting or not inviting him in for coffee.

He takes the roses, lays them on the backseat, and blindly, it seems to MC, steers his tank of a vehicle out into the Beeline. There's no traffic.

She doesn't really like the idea of leaving for breakfast at 5:30 in the morning, but he insists they have to get to this place, which is on the beach, fifty miles away—or it gets too crowded.

"Even on Sunday?" Mary Carolyn is incredulous. "I can't believe I'm doing this!"

"Oh, you are!"

"I don't know," she says again, urging him with her entire being to not lean over onto her side while he is driving. Can he even see?

"So it's the beach, at the beach?"

"That's right. Mort's House of Crab."

"Fish?"

"Well, what I'm saying is they have the best breakfast anywhere I've ever been in the world, Mrs. Jackson."

"Well, you've been a lot of places."

They're cruising out the Beeline, steadily, about forty miles an hour. MC feels more comfortable—her toes are no longer clenched inside her sneakers. She is trying to ungrind her teeth. After a bit she tells him the main problem. "I have a fear of going over bridges," she says. "My children make fun of me. I guess it's a phobia. It's like a phobia."

"Oh," he says.

"I tend to avoid beaches, Altamonte Springs, and the Gulf Coast, you know?"

"You should live in Nebraska."

"That's where you're from."

Gord plays the radio. Then he turns it off.

"Gord. Gord. I have to tell you something. I can't eat. Georgia came over—she called me last night, some big emergency to come get her. She's not in her bedroom. She then, last night this is, she's not there, where she says she will be. Then she shows up. Now she's gone. I'm worried sick."

"What happened? Slow down!"

"Anyway, the key is she is *missing*; she escaped or something. She took off, didn't leave a note, I don't know where she is—I can't leave town right now! I spent the whole night worrying about her."

"Is it the bridge thing? You hate going over bridges?"

"Please," she says, and she puts her hand over his mouth. It's a funny feeling—he is dry, like a cracker. "It's Georgia. She left last night. While I was making dinner."

"She's okay. She's with her father."

Mary Carolyn looks out the back window, half hoping to see Georgia and Oscar in CHAOS behind them. She looks down at the roses. They aren't happy being laid out in the backseat like that.

"Well, yes. Look ahead. Bridge. Big one. Let's us stop. Regroup. I need a minute to think. I'm so sorry, Gord."

"Don't give it another thought."

He seems to be missing the entire point.

They stop at the intercoastal waterway, at the foot of the bridge, and pull down to where the fishermen all park. The sand is well wet and muscled with shells.

"There's a pay phone. Call the girl's father. Put your mind to rest."

MC lunges out of the car before it stops.

The phone's coin slot is all pitted with sea salt, and her coins won't fit. She calls Buck collect. No answer. She rolls her head back, bites her tongue. There's Gord, in the boxlike car. A sharp breeze, a weird mix of cool and hot air, rushes under the bridge, off the waterway, and MC regrets leaving her sweater.

Then, she calls her own number collect—maybe Sid, or Georgia, is at the house. Nada. While the phone rings in her dark house, she examines the pilings. They are rusted—she can't believe this bridge holds traffic, she can't believe it. A truck rumbles over, and the entire structure shakes. She has read that most bridges are not completely up to code.

She tries to think of whom to call. She dials zero and thinks she could ask the police for advice.

Gord waves from the driver's seat, happy as a viburnum in flower.

The morning is developing. The sky is orchid, orange and purple and green—thick bands. Mary Carolyn brushes her hair off her face, so that the wind will all blow it in one direction, like sea grass. The salt air and fishy water envelop her, and she wishes she could fly.

"I think we'll try to give her another hour." MC sinks into the car and puts her head in her hands. "I don't know how to do this," she says.

"You do great. Teenage girls are not easy."

"Boy, you said it."

"I know."

He tells her of his days in the army corps of engineers, and the bridges, and uses words she doesn't know. It makes her want to read. It also makes her feel oddly tense, because she is waiting for the *point* to be that we all feel as though we don't always know exactly what to do in times of great stress. But that is not the point. There is no point. Gord is just talking.

"And then, when I had those blacks from the Kansas towns under me, then that was when I was telling you my wife—"

MC's eyes are closed. They are ramping up the bridge. She is gripping his arm and her armrest. Her feet float off the floor—she doesn't want to add any more pressure to the bridge.

"You feeling okay about going over, then? Look. You can practically see Mort from here!" He clears his throat again.

She's afraid he is going to put his hand on her leg. But she doesn't want to hug the side of the door, for fear it will fly open and cast her into the sea, the raging river.

"Smooth now. We're creeping forward."

"Okay, sure. I'm hanging on. I'm such a dope. My daughter laughs at me. She wants to bungee-jump off this bridge. At least she says."

MC says to herself: *I am not sure how worried to be. I feel like I am always the wrong amount of whatever it is I should be; too much this, too little that.*

When they pull into the parking lot of Mort's, just the other side of the bridge, Gord is smiling. He obviously doesn't realize they will have to go back over the bridge shortly. MC tries to not think of Georgia being attacked and left for dead, her breasts gaping in the sun, exposed, the police making unpleasant jokes. A girl was beheaded in Apopka. When was that?

"Ya hungry?"

"I'm thinking maybe pancakes, I guess." MC says. "If they have a small order."

Gord hops out, opens her door, helps her out, formally.

"We have a lot in common, Mary Cee," he says.

She tilts her head down.

"Yup. Yup, we do." The oyster shells crunch under him. He's not moving into the restaurant.

She's antsy. She can't get her breath.

How happy she is that she feels something, anything, anything at all. When she hugs him, in the parking lot of Mort's, she can feel and hear his stomach rumbling.

"I'm so happy," he says. "I can't tell you how nice this is. You are so nice to me, Mary Carolyn. You are so sweet."

She tells him she can feel his heart.

"Oh, wow," he says, and his gummy grin is wide, so wide.

Fla. Boys

I started driving early. I was twelve. I am a girl. It was not what I lived for.

At first my main fears about driving were (1) a dog would run out in front of me and I would crush it and never be able to drive again I would be so upset, and (2) my door would fly open and I would fall out and get run over by my own back wheels, my neck tangled hopelessly in the rear axle.

By the time I was fifteen, I was fairly confident on the road. My dad in the front seat, sort of conducting. My uncles, Geno and Donny, once in a while packed into the backseat, their drinks in iced tea glasses. They loaded me with compliments. We didn't see them that often.

Most often it was me driving my dad at four in the afternoon out the two-track to Amber's, where there were chickens and beer and what my father called moonshine but was regular Gordon's in regular fifths.

Other times I drove to school, and put the car in the teacher lot, and walked in through the front doors. Sometimes I drove the Trail to the ABC in the morning. Sometimes even the highway when he wanted to go downtown for a drink.

Nothing bad happened, except when we got pulled over, and then I did everything my father told me to do, and miraculously, it worked. I cried, and my father had explained we were on the way to the hospital. He kept talking, and somehow he had made his drink disappear—I still don't know how he did that. Once the cop ended up giving me money, two damp twenty-dollar bills. Figure that out.

When I was fifteen and six months, my father got me a thirty-day restricted driver's emergency license. I would get to drive him to the hospital. Then, I would take care of myself for two weeks. This time, the hospital part was true. I wasn't worried about my father.

"They take out six inches of colon, sweetie; it's nothing." His belly was pregnant with fluid—he was huge, and his skin was yellow. We sat in the kitchen drinking—I was having a beer. His little suitcase was on the dining room table. On top of his aqua pajamas, white cloudy plastic flasks, full.

The license was bigger than a normal license. It was laminated. There was no photo of me. My restrictions were printed on the back in red: (A) Operator may only drive 7:00 A.M.–7:00 P.M. (B) Forty-five miles per hour maximum speed.

The restrictions seemed dangerous. With these instructions I was a slow-moving target.

To get the license, I had driven down to the Orlando City Hall with my father. We'd moved, from a condo by my mom's house, to South Orlando, where we had a pool and palm trees and a green driveway. I drove, illegally, as I did most of the time. He liked to have his gin and tonic going, in his smoky tall glass, a cigarette dangling dangerously above the drink. That was how I learned to drive. You learn to not spill any fluid.

I'd dressed up in my favorite outfit; I was still sure there'd be a photo, and I was thrilled—I mean I actually thought this might lead to a modeling portfolio. I clasped purple pooka shells around my neck. I had a bitchin' suntan, because my father and I had a pool—in the front yard—of our Southside stucco ranch. I wore my white sundress, and I loosened the ties at the shoulders so my breasts would look bigger—you couldn't tell really, I thought, if it was the dress flipping around or my boobs. I was thinking, I will invite a guy over to the house, and we will have champagne by the pool. I was thrilled to be on my own for two weeks. My father had stocked the freezer in the garage with meat.

"Don't dawdle," my father said, and he held out his palm for the keys. I got out of the car and went to put money in the city hall meter. The palms were scratching together, their fronds like legs. *Itch, itch.*

"Don't fuck with that, I'm right here," he growled out the passenger window.

I turned on my heels and walked up the forty stairs, into the city hall. I pretended I was a lawyer. I was in stiletto Candies, red.

I gave the clerk my fat folder of papers, documenting my father's surgery, the hardship, the loss of work, and giving them a fake address, my uncles' Kissimmee ranch. Farm kids could get the Temporary even without an Emergency.

Here you go, she said.

I wanted it to be harder. I wanted my photo taken. These would be my dominant reactions to many situations for the rest of my life.

When I was a little girl, I would climb into the backseat of my father's car, late, late at night, but so bright in Florida in summer, and I would lie back there on his newspapers and bottles and the fertilizer sacks and papers and carbons, and I would pretend a man was making love to me. I don't know where I got that stuff. I guess you just know what goes where.

The next night, when he passed out on the couch, his pale, almost green gaseous belly stiff on top of him, I took his keys and sat in the giant brown Olds out in the green cement driveway, on my side, the passenger side. I had the license in my hand. My sweat was buckling the lamination. I sat out there for hours and thought of men, and how they drive women around. I didn't need to drive secretly at night, like most kids. I did all that driving during the day.

The next day my father didn't get out of bed. I swam in the lake. I was pretending I was a seal, shooting up from the white mucky bottom of Lake Conway every time a plane came over the blue lake, and barking, *orr orr orr*. Right then the Carrington boys came by in their Mercury boat and asked me if I wanted to ride around. I said no.

They sped off, and I went down to the bottom. I don't know why. Their white bathing suits, bright flags flapping in the wind, scared me, like dinner napkins and mothers and rapes and won races.

That night, I cried out in the Olds. I was so sad I hadn't gone with those Carrington boys. I started the engine, backed out of the driveway, hitting the neighbor's curb, and I drove slow and smooth as Johnny Hartman sang "My Favorite Things" on 88.4, my father's favorite station. I sang loud, and I put on his pilot sunglasses. I prowled around the Southside in the big car, pretending I was a pimp, or a Colonel or a cat or a woman with small children or a woman with no children at all.

The last night before he went in to Orange Memorial I was completely happy to sit in the driveway with my hands on my father's sticky steering wheel. It was like I was hiding, and everyone I knew had quit looking for me.

•

I was fifteen. I didn't even own a wallet yet. The Emergency license sat in my red plastic purse alone, among my lipgloss and eye shadow and concealer and tiny plastic Hallmark calendar and calculator and Troll doll, all the things I would get to keep forever.

I drove him to the grocery store. It was his last day.

"Monday dinner," I said, just to get him thinking on it. I threaded us between the cars, trolling and idling, and parked in places that weren't even really places in the Winn-Dixie parking lot. I worked around broken bottles and grocery carts and a large St. Bernard who looked to be suffering a heat stroke out by the cart corral.

"Why do you want to park in bum-fuck Egypt?" he said.

"Is there something wrong with your legs?" I said.

"As a matter of fact," he said.

He bought me everything I wanted that day, and finally I wanted some things. More makeup. A giant pink-iced angel food cake. A tiny bottle of champagne. I don't even know if it was real or play.

We stopped at the ABC, and he sat inside at the revolving bar for one hour and twelve minutes while I waited in the car, reading *Seventeen* and staring at the men who went in and out. Everything was fine except I was melting inside, I was so worried he would die of cancer. And he was. He was to have his ear cut off and six inches of colon taken out.

"I'll tell you what to worry about," he said. He was frying fish that night. Dad always made us wonderful dinners, chop suey and chicken Buck. He could do Mexican, he could do Indian, he could do steak and potatoes. Everything he cooked tasted so good.

"Thanks for making this wonderful dinner," I said, in my most unworried voice.

"Jesus, who the fuck can't cook," he said. "If you can follow directions, you can cook."

I didn't point out that he didn't follow any directions at all; he stumbled around throwing things on the counter and making an enormous mess. My job was to clean up that mess. I didn't point out that one of his refrains was "people in this world can't follow goddamn directions."

We ate out on the patio in the purple starlight. He threw his bones into the pool. Bones float sideways.

Then it was the morning of Tuesday, June 7th. I drove him to the hospital. He told me again where I was born, pointing five floors up to a dirty greenish window.

"You looked like Rocky Marciano." He always said this. He laughed in a sad way, like it was the end of something, my birth, his seeing me like Rocky.

"How much did it hurt my mother?" I wanted to say. I was having trouble keeping my eyes on the road, much less doing the circle of rotations between the road, the rearview, and the sideview. *Did she scream? Was sex worth this? Why was a baby so big? Couldn't it start off much smaller, much much smaller, something to fit in your palm, something the size of a penis, something appropriate for the woman? Couldn't we find a way to grow them out here, in the open, an easier way?*

I looked at my father, transmitting my questions to him subliminally, as always. He didn't like to be asked things, unless he asked you to ask.

"Ask me if I fucking care." "Ask me how to wire a goddamn house, I will fucking tell you. Hell, I'll fucking show you." "Ask me what you should do with your life, Georgia. Ask me."

I didn't ask him, never about her. He'd left her. I'd bounced back and forth and ended up with him. He had what he called mixed feelings. This always made me think of cement. Mixed feelings. Our lives, the product of mixed feelings.

"Turn around back. Not here. This whole part is for ambulances. Damn it."

She was married. Sid lived with them and appeared helpful. Because of Sid's various scams and freelance jobs, we rarely saw him. So who knew what was what. The only thing I knew was that one time, he stole a dead guy's garment bag from the airport. No one claimed it. It was filled with suits. He used the man's Cross pen as his own. It was a story I turned over and over in my mind. Somehow, Sid seemed imprinted with this bag, this death. And my mother seemed to have moved to a nearby friendly but inaccessible planet, with completely different atmospheric conditions. She chattered now, and didn't stop asking questions, all of them inanely kind. It was like she was on drugs. She'd gone from pained and shy to surface speed skater. I couldn't breathe or swallow when I was around any of the three of them.

This was not the day to ask my father particulars about my mother, who she was, what his theories of Sidster were. When he was in the mood, he liked to philosophize. My dad worried about the meaning of life, and the development of the lives he'd touched or crashed. I liked that. I needed that.

We were into the Emergency period. He was getting cancer out of his colon. He was getting the colon out of his system. When you live with an alcoholic, if you are fifteen, you learn quickly and sweetly. You learn that many things can be put off. You learn how to stay in a place of not-knowing. My mother, our lives, our lack of contact, it was all an uncomfortable mystery to me. You never would consider asking prognosis, odds, or how much money is there. Not-knowing. You learn to find this somewhat relaxing.

Earlier in the morning he had showed me how to fix the toilet, that creepy rusty water, the green corroded chain, and how to load his gun, those slimy shells—he didn't think there was anything else I ought to need to know. A gun and a commode is what I had to hold me through the next two weeks. Hormel tamales and fourteen frozen cube steaks.

Onions in our yard. Enough muriatic acid for the pool for a year. And the Emergency license.

I was driving perfectly, around the back of the hospital, up into the parking garage, wrapping around, not gunning the engine at this very low speed—I was going two miles an hour, not spilling a drop, even though inside I thought my father would die during this operation, I would never see him again, I would drive to his funeral with an expired Emergency license.

We didn't have the radio on. He was nervous, but he was always nervous. He always had a lot going on. He was drinking the whole way down to the hospital, long drinks out of his smoky gray glass.

He looked hard into his fist, which had just swallowed his cigarette, his eyebrows untamed wires, his complexion yellow from the colon blockage, his eyes sweating, his blue jumpsuit unzipped too far. He had gotten all skinny in the face and shoulders and legs and arms. His middle was more enormous, as if he were pregnant way past the time, like sixteen months or something.

On level three, I braked and gas-pedaled at the same time I think. My legs were all mixed up, the car chortling, my father coughing, and I wanted to just take a breather at this four-way stop; I just really wanted to stop and not think, just pause the world for a moment, a big moment. It spilled. It spilled, my father's fist, around his drink, the drink was on the floor, and ice slid around, and I lurched through the intersection and somehow the Olds was spinning, a wide circle, like how guys drive on purpose, at night, doing their donuts, sometimes. Spinning, and then Buck socked me in the throat. He socked me hard. The parked cars slipped past my windows. We lurched on through. I could make no noise. Up to level five.

I concentrated on the burning on my neck and the red golf cart in front of me, with its pails of paint stacked like white heads.

"Sorry about that," he said. He had ochre eyes, always wet. "Get going. Now, get going. You're going to get rear-ended. And in a couple of hours I'm getting out six inches of my colon. Get the vehicle out of the goddamn intersection. Go up to the top."

My hands tingled on the steering wheel, my stomach whooshing. This was pretty much my constant state.

"We oughta get 'em to put it in formaldehyde so we can display my contribution on the mantel. What do you think about that as a conversation piece, baby?" My dad smiled, and you could tell he was seeing a crowd of people around our mantel, and all of us talking and laughing.

I pulled up to the Admitting doors at the top of the parking garage. There was no plan.

"Just let me out," he said. He didn't have the suitcase. Standing in the sun, he drained the rest of the bottle, a jug of gin he had in the backseat. There wasn't a lot left.

"Dad," I was going to say, "are they going to cut you open? Is it going to hurt? Will you know when they are inside you? Will you not be able to feel then?" But my throat hurt from where he hit me, and I just turned on the radio—I didn't know the tune—and he walked into the building.

I waited, idling for a few minutes, like moms do when they drop you off at school or dance lessons.

How do you know what gets inside of you? Why was I born? How could you ever figure out something like that? How could you not? I wanted to drive into the lake behind the hospital. By way of a cure.

I didn't know much about cancer. What it was. It seemed like stones. I knew about guns and toilets and making drinks, mimosas, Molotov cocktails, his favorites. I knew about butt-fucking. My father's pornography collection was vast and specific.

I didn't know any people who had died. I didn't know that many people.

•

My dad didn't come back out. He hadn't forgotten anything, not anything that he had, anyway.

He'd said the cancer of the colon thing was nothing. It was good to get rid of your excess colon. You had two hundred feet of the stuff. What he was getting rid of was just excess. It wasn't anything. He said that about everything—him not going to work, finding me still asleep in the back of the car in the afternoon, stunned in the sun, the Florida room flooding and the television in water sparking, cops at the door at five in the afternoon, a woman trying to stab him on our patio on his birthday, me drinking beer and floating in the pool so that I could drown. It wasn't anything. None of it was anything.

I believed that I was going to be okay while I had the Emergency License.

I circled down out of the parking garage, pretending I was twenty-seven years old. I put on some more lipgloss and my father's sunglasses. I changed the radio station to WDIZ, Rock 100, and it was Van Halen, and I knew the song by heart. "Pretty Woman." Ah, I said. "Oh baby." That was a shame, because those words hung around in the car with me.

I drove down the Orange Blossom Trail, with the radio on super loud. I was looking for a drive-thru liquor window. I was going to try out the credit card I had been given by my pops.

The Olds was chugging funny. I wondered if spinning out, if losing it back there in the parking garage, had that hurt the car? He'd told me to take the car to Earl if I had any trouble. Earl at the Shell station was always trying to feel me. Earl had a cot behind the Coke cooler and a mattress in his Rescue Van. The misnomer of the century.

"Hey, baby, you sure look wonderful," a guy on a motorcycle yelled into my open window at the red light on Bumby.

"Oh, thank you," I said. It was so funny to me how no one knew what you had just done.

•

I wanted to use up this part of my life driving on the highway. I decided to take the Beeline to the beach, to Daytona Beach. I would just sit there in the sun. I was wearing diaper shorts—those shorts that are printed with parrots and palm trees, of thin cotton, that you wrap up between your legs, and then the ties wrap around your waist. And my pink tube top. I looked pretty cute and skinny and tan and significantly twenty-seven. I could just sit on the beach on my diaper shorts, and if they got wet, I had on great underwear; that could be mistaken for my bathing suit, and I could drive home in that easily.

The shins always lost their color first. I would get my shins back even with my arms and thighs. The tan was important.

I curdled up the I-4 access ramp and took the Beeline exit, a clover-leaf that I handled like an expert, and I loaded myself onto the highway. It felt like roller skating, going this fast after having been limited to low speeds for all these weeks. The rumble in the engine disappeared, and I started breathing better. I sped up. I went a little faster than the speed limit, like everybody else. Something my father would never let me do.

Highway 50 draws a neat straight line across Florida, like a belt from the sea to the gulf. It was Tuesday in the middle of the afternoon. It was hot and salty, and the palms and the crotons and the oleanders planted along the sides of the highway looked scratchy and tired and somewhat poisonous, which they were. The sky was a washed-out blue, and I had tears in my eyes. I liked my highway—no other cars. I liked my lane. It made a rhythm like my heart.

I headed to the sea, steering with one hand. I powered down all the windows to one-half.

But then I changed my mind. I would go back and make myself a mimosa and sit in the pool, keep an eye on the Olds, and watch the stars come out and reheat some of the chicken Buck in the microwave and then watch the Clint Eastwood channel. I didn't want to get stuck at the beach hungry and then have to drive back home in the dark. I didn't want to get stuck anywhere at all.

I pulled over, to a Fat Joe's. Gas. I needed gas. You always need gas if you have an Olds. They are true gas hogs. But I didn't want to buy gas at that juncture. I wanted to go right home and reset my head, break through the walls.

Highway 50 had quickly become peculiar to me. I couldn't tell which way was back to my dad's house, couldn't tell which way went on out to the ocean or the gulf. I went a ways and then, no, wrong way. To get back I had to go east. I looped around on the median, ten miles back the other way, and then I would do it scared all over again. I kept passing the Fat Joe's. There were no signs that were useful to me. I must have turned around ten times. I was lost on a straight line.

I was lost on a straight line.

The town back over in the marsh was Christmas. In Christmas, Florida, a town of 1,322, I was lost. I was lost, crying, then screaming. My throat hurt on both sides, like I had a scalpel there in my neck. The same kind of Florida scrub—palmettos and sword bushes passed in my windows. I couldn't read the sky. I couldn't figure it.

One thing I remembered from living with my mother: the death scream. It's just a scream you can do when you are upset and you want people to back off, to give you some room to work in. I screamed her scream. Then I was shaking the car by the steering wheel, by the neck it seemed—everything was coming loose, the sky was one big blue eye and I could hardly see, soaked, red, a puff—I let go and screamed, thinking I'd fall. My dad's Olds rolled into a ditch.

My head didn't hit the windshield when the car banked and rocked over, so I slammed it against the windshield myself. It didn't crack. The jug of empty gin rollicked up to my feet, lay there like an accusation, a destiny. I pitched it out the window.

I was so wet between my legs I thought I had had an accident or a female emergency, but it was just sweat. I thought, well, the backseat. A little sleep. But I was too sideways, and I couldn't get back there. I had to sit on my own door. I had no idea which way to go. I wanted to walk down the highway with the steering wheel. That would be funny. Straight to the hospital, please. I just wanted to share a room with my father. We could be together now.

I waited. No blood. I was just soaked with sweat. I kept looking at my face and head in the rearview mirror. No one came. I turned the rearview mirror to me so I could stare at myself without having to crane my neck. No contusions arose to the surface like lovely rose tattoos.

It was so hot. No cars passed me. Would I be a person walking into Christmas? I was sticking to the vinyl bad. It was hard not to think about Earl and his creepy van and my dad and his colon like a sausage in brine on our mantel. You can't get stuff like that out of your head unless you are willing to sacrifice years of memory around it, and at my age, that would pretty much wipe me out.

The pine trees were only about a foot outside the ditch. Their needles were so green, so dark, they seemed like ink up there, through my dad's window.

"Shut up, trees," I said. I spoke out loud. "Good-bye," I said, and turned the rearview mirror around so as to face them, those scaly trees, and not me anymore. "Bad bye" I shouted. "How don't you do!"

Nothing seemed wrong, except the crowd was missing, and I knew my dad had been asked to lie down and breathe in a blue gas, and he was not thinking about me. There were dirty magazines at home on the dining room table. There was porn in the suitcase and both bathrooms. So I needed a boyfriend somewhat older than the Carrington boys and their innocent red boat with its sharp white flags.

Keep it on the road. I knew what he meant by that now.

In my next dream he lived. I died because I went off the road and that was the last thing. No one would know! This was my constant fix. I wanted to live in order to tell people, but in order to be interesting my good stories required my death.

I started screaming again, out loud or not, I don't know. Three big green Publix trucks passed fast and I felt my car wiggle and shudder, even though it was locked into mud. You know how some people start laughing to keep from crying, or so they say; I've never seen anybody do that. I do the opposite.

In a ditch, in an Olds Delta 88, in Christmas, Florida, so sweaty I am smelling like formaldehyde, I started howling harder maybe than I have ever howled, and I have howled, because everything takes so long when you are kid. I started screaming so hard my whole body hurt. I tried to rip my shorts, but there wasn't a way to get a good grip. I was wet, and huge mucus was everywhere. I was screaming red screams and scratching my face. No one came. There weren't that many people in Christmas. A cougar escaped from Circus Land two weeks ago, and they hadn't caught it yet. It was kind of a flat jungle. There aren't that many people in Florida. I know it must seem like it if you just see Florida on television, but the crowds here are clustered in pockets. It is mostly trees, cows, bushes, and bugs and more field scrub, a cougar or three. Not that many people. Fat Joe's. I didn't see the cougar.

I got out by opening up the passenger door, my dad's door now, and climbed out like from a box. Like the lady out of the cake. I said "Hello" when I got out. The car was so hot, like an eye on your stove. Man. My thighs sizzled. My diaper shorts were scooched up into my butt. Adjusting, I slid off of the car. It was hurt pretty bad. It made me think of an abandoned jungle gym, the brown knot of it.

I hopped down into the reeds.

I wiped my face off on the soft weeds, cattails, in the ditch. I threw my Emergency license and then my whole purse into the hyacinths because I would never ever be driving again. No one could make me.

I was lost, ankle-deep in humus. It was noon, and the sky just kept going higher and higher, like each breath I took puffed my clean blue blanket off of me a bit more.

I felt naked in my tube top and my shorts. They were so short when you sat down it was like a bathing suit up around your thighs, tight and into the skin.

On my way up to the highway, I saw a baby alligator in the water in the ditch with my car, sunning on a stick in the muck—they always look like they are smiling, and I felt just like him. I wanted to slip into his mud with him, stay small and soft and have little bright teeth like that.

He couldn't remember a thing. He couldn't know why my car was lodged like a spaceship on his nest. He couldn't care less. He wasn't even grinning.

It's like I was in a fog, but without the fog. Not that I was slow. I went to a special school called PEP. You had to be smart, and you had to have some kind of problem. The same kids had always known me. One had a rod in her back, Sara. She'd been my best friend since I was seven, she said all the time to everyone. She made me wear her jewelry and her flower blouses over my halters. The others that went to PEP were all boys, brilliant nerds with epilepsy or hemophilia or something else like hyperactivity or a habit of touching themselves, something that didn't show up to us or seem at all important. Me and Sara tied their shoes together while they did enormous and tormented math problems. We were supposed to teach each other in PEP. Sara and I taught the boys how to love us, how to be our lovers. I did all of this without speaking or remembering. The boys taught us how to balance checkbooks and exactly what the gonads were capable of. We had to translate Dolly Parton's measurements into metric. They were interested in learning that kind of thing. They liked the idea of taking pi out to the millionth digit, working it out on rolls of toilet paper. They got into fist fights over infinity and the Big Bang and the size of the largest mammalian penis.

"It's not the elephant. It's that guy from Austria in the *Guinness Book of World Records*."

"It's a shark."

"Well, how are we defining largest? Length, bulk, circumference, or total cubic volume when erect?"

"You have to factor in flaccid weight, or you are an asshole, butt face."

Blue whale, I didn't say.

You will write us a love letter every morning, first thing when you get to school, okay, boys? Sara had them all churning the stuff out. Now, we move to roses, she said. She actually said that. Next, promise rings! We'll make 'em, and you just give them to us when I say.

It was a great school.

We were allowed to write on the walls and to play the stock market in theory. The teacher talked on the phone all day, selling real estate.

I played along, but I wasn't happy to receive presents from Sara's hostages. It didn't feel like love; it felt like school. I just wanted to cheat.

I wasn't really interested in anything except the film room down the hall because it was dark. There was only one movie in all those tin circles—*Michelangelo: Tragic Genius*. I was allowed to go there on Fridays and only if Sara came with me. We watched it and watched it and watched it on the wall. None of the boys were allowed in there with us. It was too much focus on the breast, Mr. Rose said, with Michelangelo, the tragic genius. I loved the stealing corpses part. I just loved it that you had to have an arm in order to draw an arm.

All those boys liked me, and they made me the Queen of Dogs before school let out. They would follow me around the PEP classroom on their all fours and bark, and I spoke my secret language—"Zimba Marton. Cray Cray." They went crazy rolling at my feet. Sara got mad when I was made Queen, especially at her fiancé, John Trumble, rolling around and barking and salivating at my feet, the one she loved best, but you know she'd never marry him. She was just playing eighth grade. She would be different next year.

Now Sara Sims was the type who would go over to Fat Joe's and call the police, I think. She wasn't allowed to ride motorcycles or wear bikinis because of the rod in her back. She was a police caller. But I was scared to call. I was always a criminal-feeling girl. Like when the coffee money was stolen from the teacher's lounge at PEP I wondered: could it have been me? It wasn't, but I always worried.

I creeped over to that Fat Joe's, making it seem like I was just walking on in from any old direction.

I cried by the pumps. Maybe I would just get in someone's car. I walked up to the freestanding booth with the money woman in it and pulled my shorts down better. They were hiked and wrinkled and all wet. I couldn't see the car, and that was good. It was just below the horizon. Like the yellow alligator, I couldn't see what happened.

The woman in the booth at the pumps gave me some questions and tried to be helpful.

"Where you trying to go, sweetie?"

I explained that I lived in South Orlando, and I had a car, not far away, and I was just lost.

"Oh, sugar, it's okay, you want a Coke?" I didn't. She gave me directions to my subdivision. It was just a line she drew, a line that was also an arrow, and she put an "X" where my house was, at the end of the line. It angered me, this map. It was not what I needed. How was I supposed to figure out which way to hold that arrow. You could turn it an infinite number of directions.

"No, thanks," I said. My throat hurt like it had had something jammed into it.

I just wandered off across the parking lot, over to the line of pumps where truckers filled up their tanks. I mouthed the words "taxi cab" into the sky, and then I started humming Van Halen. Little bit of a dance, a sexy dance.

I stepped in front of a large red truck with a man filling two gas tanks, one on each side. His engine was running. This was illegal. I stood in front, aligning myself with where he stood in the back, looking into his grille, which had a piece of a bird, a pigeon, caught in it. The wing was fine, but the rest was a smeary mess. I looked at the road and could tell I wouldn't ever know which way to go.

I said I was lost.

"Are you lost, girl?"

"My horse ran away," I said. "Our best paint." I fell onto him and tried to cry. I wondered if maybe I should ask him to take me to a hospital, an orderly well-run mental hospital, but then how could I pick my dad up in two weeks, how could I keep the toilet on track?

His name was Michael it said on his shirt in red writing. He had hair like the fake icicles that hung on the gas pumps, dried out white hair, salt and sun hair, but he was young. He had all kinds of deer horns and fish bait cartons and turtle shells laid out across his dashboard. I thought of my egg. All this stuff. All this life that he had, all this that never spilled. I sat on the edge of the sofalike seat in his truck while he paid and got me a Coke and him a carton of Marlboros.

"I can't find my way home." I had let the map blow off, even though there was no wind. I had no pockets. No change of clothes. I had no purse, no bra, not a dime, even the Emergency license was not on me. My long blonde hair was all around my hot pink tube top, like waves.

"Well, what's your name?"

"Georgia," I told him. "Like the state."

He smiled. "Where are you trying to get?" His lips were thin and white, and his eyes were like horse's eyes, big and brown.

I liked it that he didn't ask where I was coming from.

"I don't know," I said. I knew this was the most radical thing I had done, even more radical than putting my dad's Olds in that deep wet ditch. It was a lie. A public lie. I thought it was sad that my lying debut had to take place at Fat Joe's in Christmas. But I was driving off the road, fast and hard. I had already spilled.

That afternoon, late, red, orange, and blue, in Room 2-7, in a hotel by the beach, a Daytona 500 trucker's hotel with no name, two stories, and long black railings wrapping around the second floor like a small prison or a Spanish condo, an odd long hour away from Orange Memorial Hospital, Michael showed me how much money he had on him. We went through his boots, five hundred dollars in each. His wallet on a chain, pictures of kids, one-hundred-dollar bills behind each of them, and a one-thousand-dollar bill in a secret pocket. We went through his shirt together, and there were secret inside places with one-hundred-dollar bills.

I wanted to lay it all out on the baby round table and get all of the heads facing the same way. I pushed some of the bills toward each other, a little family of Franklins.

"Don't even fuck with me, not once, or I will kill you."

"Thank you," I said. "I won't." I felt I was doing well.

I got under the covers. I pulled the white sheet up to my neck and lay there with my arms at my sides. This made me think of my father. I smiled. This was my life! The brown scratchy bedspread smelled like cigarette smoke, and when Michael sat down on the end of the bed, the smoke smell puffed and made me cough. He leaned forward, lit a cigarette with his silver lighter, and changed the channels on the television.

"You sure are quiet, girl," he said. He didn't look back at me. He had cartoons on really loud. "Let's get ourselves hungry," he said.

He put the cigarette in his mouth backward and pulled his shirt, a button shirt, over his head. His slim wrists slipped through the cuffs, and he threw the inside-out shirt on the television and kicked the cigarette back out. The arm of the shirt draped over the cartoons. He slid his belt out and said, "What are you lookin' at?" in a mean voice, but he was smiling. "Your hair looks so beautiful, gold on white," he said. "Against the sheets. My God," he said. "This is not what I was expecting when I woke up this morning. Angel hair."

"Where do you live?" I said. He turned up the air conditioner.

"To block out noise," he said, and I didn't follow up or imagine or do anything except take my diaper shorts off under the covers and push them with my feet down to the end of the bed, under the spread, where things were heavy and tight.

"You never fucked a nigger, I hope," he said.

"No one," I whispered to him when he lay down next to me, on top of the spread. I could hardly move. I could feel my legs sweating and between my legs spreading. The light in the room was blue, and although it was stuffy and close and strange, I liked it. I liked being away from the car, far from Amber's, far from the freezer of chuck steak, the hospital. I liked not having my purse.

"I wish I had a photograph of you," I said.

"Why don't you get out from under there and let me look at you," he said. "Let me see a little bit more of ya." His voice was soft and sweet. He was watching television, the part you could see around the sleeve, while he talked to me, but it wasn't like my dad. He wanted to see me.

"No," I said. Michael looked at me then, his white icicle hair didn't move, but he did. He took me in his arms and laughed. "You get down in here with me," I said. I started kicking and kicking the heavy brown spread, making smoke smells puff into the room, and I got the stuff over him at last, and I said, "Let me take off your pants."

"What? Are you my angel?" he said, and I was glad I was under the covers, in the brown tent, because I would have started laughing or maybe I would have burst into tears had I seen his face when he said *that*.

I unzipped his pants slowly, and then I started scooting them down his slim hips, over his funny bent hipbones. This is much harder to do than you would think. You have to really yank. It's nothing like a doll, which is smooth and plastic and purely dry. His skin looked older and his hair was blonde, all the way up his legs, curlier and curlier as you got to his gray underwear. The smell was of acid and lemons and sulfur. It was like playing tent with my brother when we were little, except for that complex smell.

I could not tell if he had a hard-on or not. I started kissing his knees, pulling the hairs with my teeth, and licking and kissing the skin, which was salty and fearless. I worked my way up to the above-the-knee.

His hands came down under the covers like two cheerful squids. I was happy to feel them. He kneaded my butt and stroked me like I was a car, then a bird, then a saddle.

I was so wet it was like I had my period, and it was gross and strange and wonderful under those covers. I could hardly breathe, so I sounded like I was panting with pleasure, which I thought was a good thing.

"Are you my angel? Am I going to fall in love with you?" Woody Woodpecker made his famous noise, and it was like Woody was talking to me. I had my eyes open and could only see the wall. I was licking the white scratchy sheet. I was numb from the waist down. I couldn't feel anything. My feet were sweating buckets, though. I could tell that.

"I hope not," I said as softly as I could talk, which was very, very soft.

We had shrimp dinner down at the pier late that night, and he bought me a rose from the girl with them in her white plastic basket.

"She's gorgeous," the girl said. "And you're going to get ten years.

They have laws, Tackett," she said, laughing. I had this feeling they knew each other, but I had that feeling about every single set of people I encountered ever since I got my memory back. I liked the rose. It had black edges, and it was a tight bud.

It would never open. I knew that. Just looking at it.

"That will open up real nice in the next few days," he said. He was building River Country, part of Disney. He got paid in cash at the end of every day. He had cement poisoning, and I felt sure I was going to get it on my legs too. He had a woman on his crew. He wouldn't be able to hire me on. There were too many problems with this one woman. She couldn't carry two buckets. She was willing to make two trips, but it wasn't fair. The men all hated her ways.

"I know what an Allen key is," I said. "I can fix a toilet. I know I could be very useful at River Country."

"Oh, you could be useful," Tackett said, and he put three shrimps tails into his mouth and crunched them in. "Ah," he said. I thought, the joke is on me. But I didn't care. I wanted anything. Just to have more to think about than my dad, that life. People always are saying teenagers are difficult and crazy. We just want something other than the trouble we have.

We sat on the mess of bedcovers like we were in a nest. He was skinny without his clothes, a true stick. Like my dad without the pregnant belly, but this man was hard, whip thin, yellow-eyed, but a hard yellow, not that watery yellow. We watched cartoons on television for a long time, not talking. I put on his blue work shirt and snapped it up to the top of my neck. He made me take it off and go shower and dry off really good before he let me put it back on. He didn't say anything about the way I handled things. Maybe it had gone okay. It was easy to forget. It was so easy to know that things had always been this way.

He fell asleep with the television on at 10:33 P.M. I smelled him while he slept. The ceiling had a stain on it in the exact shape of the sausage-curled head of Marie Antoinette.

Sometime late in the night, the cartoons had turned to a black-and-white movie that didn't have any cars in it, just women who yelled out all these beautiful sentences at the men in a tiny office, big women in suits with big buttons, yelling, but in the most sexy way you could imagine, like trumpets, many notes all spilling out at once—it was wonderful but it was too many words. I kept fearing a car would come on screen, or a car commercial, or even a horse-drawn carriage. I couldn't understand who was who or what the point was.

Michael Tackett was sleeping like a stick would sleep. Stiff and straight with his arms at his sides. Not a leaf stirred. I got up quick like a snake and put on his jeans. They had so much stuff on them. Dirt and writing and clots of cement. I felt like a building in progress. White streaks of caulk and sand in the pockets. I emptied his pockets. I didn't want to get killed.

I didn't want anything to happen. I didn't want one single moment anywhere in the world to go forward. Not because I was so happy, but because it seemed this was a good place to stop. Everything as yet undiscovered but completely changed—that was how I wanted to stay but that isn't a way that can stay.

The door made a sucking sound as it locked behind me. I had the feeling I was leaving something behind, but I realized I was always going to have that feeling. That was the car, that was my dad, that was my dinner, and that was my stomach. That was my memory block, that was my brother with a dead man's suits, making money, living with our mother and her terrible husband, that was the Emergency license. I walked outside, tiptoeing on the AstroTurf into the parking lot.

It could have been anywhere in the whole world of Florida, I thought. The light was my same old lonely no-lover backseat of the car light at way past midnight in my dad's driveway light. The ROOMS $20 SEA PEARL L UNGE OPEN sign blinked in gold and peach letters, and I looked back at the motel, all those dark windows like a hospital. Down the strip I could see more neon problems. BUG BOY. IMPER GARDEN.

As I walked away from the hotel, his truck, down to the highway, I thought—everyone is going to be able to see me now. I am no longer invisible.

Right after he drifted off, he had started rolling his lips, saying "Shelley, Shelley, Shelley," over and over. It was hard to tell if he was mad at her, having sex with her, or she was driving, or what. I knew she would be the mother of the kids in his wallet, the hundred-dollar bill kids. Then later he was humming emotionlessly.

He'd told me things about women, and I kept thinking of those things, those shapes, those quantities, those colors, those holes, those words he said, all he knew.

I worked toward the highway where trucks were passing with the same noise that I always felt in my stomach, the whooshing. In a while, those trucks, they would pass by the yellow shiny baby alligator and my dad's yellow car in the ditch, as they closed in on Orlando. I started walking that way. The pavement was still hot from yesterday and my sandals were already wet and salty from my sweaty feet. The pines were all inky and sharp and salty alongside me. I touched my face—it had lines deep into it, from the coarse sheets, scratching. I smelled like cigarettes. His pants, now my pants, shifted around my body as I walked, like in a denim barrel, chafing. His shirt felt like a pelt on me.

I felt like my self was a vital organ beating, somehow staying alive inside an ancient husk that was not my own. My hair: stuck to itself. A truck's horn blasted me off of the highway, like it was the first sound I ever heard, the siren I had been waiting for all this time. It was a good kind of frightened to death.

The road, that straight line, was a geometry lesson. The air, its salt making me a kind of chemical reaction I cannot even describe. That new space inside of me.

It scared me, all of it. As much as the thought of the next thing.

About the Author

Born and raised in Orlando, Florida, **Heather Sellers** received a Ph.D. in Writing from Florida State University. She currently lives in Holland, Michigan, where she's an associate professor of English at Hope College, and a Poet-in-the-Schools. Her work has appeared in the *Indiana Review, New Virginia Review, The Hawaii Review, The Chattahoochee Review, The Women's Review of Books*, and *Sonora Review*. Her story "Fla. Boys" is anthologized in *New Stories from the South, 1999: The Year's Best*. Recently she received a 2000–2002 fellowship from the National Endowment for the Arts.

David Greenwood